"*Mandy, I'm sure* ⬛⬛⬛⬛⬛⬛⬛ *excellent manager. I* ⬛⬛⬛⬛⬛⬛⬛⬛⬛ *this way.*"

Her lips quivered for a split second before she nodded. She opened her mouth to say something, but all that came out was a squeak.

"If you need some time off, let me know, okay?"

Her face looked stricken. "Why would I need time off?"

"I'm just saying. . ."

"I don't."

She took a step back and slammed into the corner of the wall. Tony instinctively reached for her as she rubbed her shoulder.

"I'm fine," she said softly before glancing at his hand resting on her arm.

He quickly pulled his hand back and shoved it into his pocket. "That's fine. I just wanted to let you know it's okay if you need time to think about things."

There wasn't even the hint of a smile on her pretty face as she stood there staring at him with those wide, long-lash-framed hazel eyes.

Tony didn't want to torture her, so he added, "After I get acclimated to the place, I'll need to start interviewing for another full-time photographer. Since you'll be training the person, I'd like for you to participate."

She didn't say a word, so he took off for the office. This had been much more difficult than he'd anticipated.

He closed the door behind him and hesitated as he looked around the room. Mandy had all but made the space her own.

DEBBY MAYNE has been a freelance writer all her adult life, starting with slice-of-life stories in small newspapers then moving on to parenting articles for regional publications and fiction stories for women and girls. She has been involved in all aspects of publishing—from the creative side, to editing a national health magazine, to freelance proofreading for several book publishers. Her belief that all blessings come from the Lord has given her great comfort during trying times and gratitude for when she is rewarded for her efforts.

Books by Debby Mayne

HEARTSONG PRESENTS
HP625—Love's Image
HP761—Double Blessing
HP785—If the Dress Fits
HP869—Noah's Ark
HP889—Special Mission

Portrait
of Love

Debby Mayne

Heartsong Presents

Thanks to Jennifer Fleahman with the Wheeling, West Virginia, Chamber of Commerce, and Margaret Prager at Suzanne's Bridal Shop for helping me with some of the facts about the city.

A note from the Author:
I love to hear from my readers! You may correspond with me by writing:

Debby Mayne
Author Relations
PO Box 721
Uhrichsville, OH 44683

ISBN 978-1-60260-906-8

PORTRAIT OF LOVE

All scripture quotations, unless otherwise indicated, are taken from the HOLY BIBLE, NEW INTERNATIONAL VERSION®. NIV®. Copyright © 1973, 1978, 1984 by International Bible Society. Used by permission of Zondervan. All rights reserved.

All of the characters and events in this book are fictitious. Any resemblance to actual persons, living or dead, or to actual events is purely coincidental.

Our mission is to publish and distribute inspirational products offering exceptional value and biblical encouragement to the masses.

PRINTED IN THE U.S.A.

one

More than twenty elementary-aged children swarmed Mandy Pruitt the instant she snapped the last picture. She laughed as she handed out the candy she'd promised. A group of moms had gotten together and brought their homeschooled children for their fall "class" photo.

The smallest of the children, a boy with floppy red hair and big green eyes, touched the camera. "Can we see the picture, Miss Mandy?"

She placed one hand on his shoulder and gestured for the other children to come around behind her with the other. "If you're very still, I'll show you what I have here. It'll look a little different after it's developed."

Mandy enjoyed her job of being a children's photographer at the Small World Portrait Studio on Market Street in Wheeling, West Virginia. A year ago, jobs were scarce, so she'd resorted to walking up and down Market Street, handing out copies of her résumé to anyone who'd take one. The former photographer had just walked out the day before, and the manager was stuck snapping pictures of unruly children.

As soon as she'd walked into the studio, one of the children in the Sunday school class she taught at church recognized her. "Miss Mandy!"

"Hey, Bailey!"

"What are you doing here?" Bailey had glanced around behind her. "Are you getting your picture took?"

"No," she'd told him. "I'm not getting my picture *taken*. I'm here to apply for a job."

When the manager saw her instant rapport with the pint-sized set, he hired her on the spot. "All we have to do is a background check, and you've got yourself a job photographing kids," he told her. "I'll put a rush on it, and you'll hear back from me in the next couple of days."

"Um. . ." Her mindless scattering of résumés had landed her a job she had no idea how to do. "I'm not exactly an experienced photographer." She'd been thinking more along the lines of receptionist since her degree in business didn't seem to matter.

He'd snickered. "That's fine. We train our photographers."

"Are you sure?"

The manager rocked back on his heels and studied her with a narrowed gaze. "Do you want a job or not?"

"Oh, yes, of course I do."

"Good." The man smiled. "As soon as we have the required background check in, I'll call, and you can start right away. I'll teach you how to use the equipment. Shouldn't take more than a day or two."

The squirminess of the children now surrounding her jolted her back to the moment. "Miss Mandy, can I have another piece of candy? Tyler took mine."

Mandy leveled the tallest boy with a stern gaze. "Tyler, keep your hands to yourself." She reached into the bag and pulled out another piece of candy for the girl. "Here ya go, Mackenzie. Why don't you save it for later?"

Mackenzie nodded and turned toward the waiting room mothers. "Mommy, looky what Miss Mandy gave us."

After the children left, Mandy went to the front desk and checked the appointment book. She didn't have another sitting for a couple of hours, but she was the only person in the studio, and she couldn't leave since they took walk-ins.

❧

Tony Mancini stood directly across the street from the studio and watched the pretty woman with the short blond hair and expressive eyes work her magic. He'd been told what a dynamo Mandy Pruitt was. If this was Mandy, her reputation didn't do her justice. She was a magician as far as he could tell. As the children filed out of the studio, they all waved and hollered their good-byes, while she smiled and waved back. After they were gone, she didn't drop the smile, but he saw her shoulders lift and fall in what appeared to be a deep sigh. The woman obviously enjoyed her job.

Tony didn't want to manage a studio, but he'd been warned when he first left and joined the army after college. His mother's brother Edward had always wanted his own son, Ricco, and nephew, Tony, to take over the company, but at that time, it wasn't what Tony had wanted. Things had changed. His father had passed away, and Tony had gotten out of the army. Now he'd have to do his time and prove his commitment to the family, starting at the store level.

Movement in the studio captured his attention once again. Mandy had the phone at her ear while she jotted something down. He watched as her expression changed. Tony decided it was time to quit standing on the sidewalk staring and go on inside. He squared his shoulders, set his jaw, and headed for the entrance.

Mandy glanced up as he entered. "May I help you?"

Tony stopped at the counter and nodded. "Yes, I'm Tony Mancini, and I'll be working with you." He pulled out his company ID and showed it to her.

She frowned. "I just found out you were coming. Sorry I didn't have more time to prepare." Her voice cracked, and she stopped talking. "Ever since Parker left, it's just been me and a couple of part-timers. I wish someone had told me before today I was getting help."

"I'm not just here to help out," he said before she buried herself any further. She obviously didn't know he was related to the owners. He resented having to take this job, but he didn't want to take it out on her. "I'm the new manager."

She blinked as the surprise registered on her face. She didn't look any happier than he felt. "Did you come from another Small World studio?"

He shook his head. "No, I just finished a few weeks of crash training at the home office, and they sent me here."

"Oh." She looked down, and her shoulders sagged.

"But I have photography experience. I was a photographer back in college, and I did a little stringing for newspapers on the side, but it was mostly journalistic work."

She didn't even try to smile when she looked back up at him. "Like car wrecks and stuff?"

He couldn't help but grin, in spite of the tension. "Yeah, something like that."

"Then you should do just fine."

At least she had a sense of humor.

ॐ

The one thing that annoyed her most about the Small World company was how they never let the store personnel know their next move. As annoyed as she was, she didn't want to risk her job, so she forced a smile.

"Oh, by the way, my name is Mandy Pruitt, and I've been here about a year."

His instant smile was warm, and she wanted to like him. "Nice to meet you, Mandy Pruitt." He extended his hand.

She wiped her palm on the side of her slacks before taking Tony's. His handshake was firm and quick.

"Mind if I take a look around?" he asked.

"C'mon, let me give you a tour of the place." She turned and walked toward the back, hoping he'd follow. The soft sound of footsteps behind her let her know he wasn't far behind. Suddenly, she heard a thumping sound, so she spun around in time to see him catch himself after nearly tripping over a stuffed animal. "Sorry," she said as she bent over to pick it up. "Kids leave things—"

He held up his hands. "Don't worry about it."

Their gazes locked, and her voice stuck in her throat. She quickly glanced away.

"Nice," he said, breaking the silence. "It looks just like the studio in the home office."

"It is." When she met his gaze again, she saw a flash of something—concern, maybe?

Tony opened his mouth to say something, when the phone rang. He nodded to the chirping receiver in her hand. "Don't let me keep you from your work."

Mandy pushed the TALK button and lifted the phone to her ear as Tony added some distance between them. "Small World, this is Mandy. How may I help you?"

"I'm stranded, and I don't know what to do. Mom said to call you."

It sounded like her sister. "Christina?"

"Yeah, Joe told me he didn't want anything to do with me anymore, and I couldn't get an acting job, so here I am, stuck in LA, no job, no boyfriend, and I can't pay my rent."

Christina had the worst timing possible. "Do you have a way to come to West Virginia?"

"No, I'm flat broke." She sniffled. "I really wanna come home. I should have listened to you and Dad about how hard it was to make a living in Hollywood."

Mandy only paused for a second before making a decision. "I'll order you a ticket, and you can pick it up at the airport."

"Thanks, Mandy. I promise I'll pay you back."

"Ssh, don't worry about that now, hon. I know you'd do the same for me. I'll call you after I book your flight."

"Can you do it now? I don't have a place to stay tonight. I—I've been evicted."

"Um. . ." Mandy glanced up at Tony, who'd once again backed away. "Sure." After Mandy hung up, she gave Tony an apologetic look. "I have a family situation."

"Better handle it then. I'm not going anywhere."

She made a beeline for the front desk to book Christina's flight. She felt Tony's presence as he joined her.

Mandy was embarrassed. "I don't do this kind of thing often, but my sister is stranded in California, and I have to buy her a ticket home."

Tony grinned. "The two of you must be close. Have you always gotten along?"

"If you don't count the childish squabbles we used to have in the backseat on long family car trips, yes. We're very close."

"Good. I'll just look around some more while you take care of this." Still smiling, he turned and left.

As Mandy went to the airline Web site, she thought about how nice Tony seemed to be—or was at least trying to be. If she'd met him anywhere but work, she would have wanted to find out more about him—like whether or not he was a Christian, and if so, was he married? But as a co-worker, the married part didn't matter because she had no intention of having an office romance.

It only took her a couple of minutes to book Christina's flight and make a brief phone call to let her know. As soon as Mandy finished her family business, she joined Tony.

"So what do you think?" she asked.

"Looks like you've done an excellent job of keeping this place running. I heard you haven't had a manager in more than a month."

Mandy wasn't about to tell him she was applying for the manager position. Last time she'd brought it up to Ricco, the corporate regional manager, she'd been advised to wait until it was posted companywide.

"Are you always here with your part-timers?" he continued.

She shook her head. "Not always, but they're both very good and reliable. I can leave either of them alone, but during the busy times, I try to schedule two people." She paused and made a face. "I'm here as much as I can be, though."

"That must be challenging." He rubbed his chin as he turned and scoped everything out. "Now that I'm here, I hope you're able to relax and maybe take some time off."

"I'm relaxed."

He nodded toward the white knuckles of her hands folded in front of her. "Oh yeah?"

"I'm fine," she said as she dropped her hands to her side, her voice tight and squeaky. She cleared her throat. "I'm a very organized person."

He studied her for several seconds before nodding. "That's nice."

The way he looked at her was unsettling. "I, uh. . .I need to go back to the front desk. Let me know if you need anything."

"I'll be up there in a few minutes. Ricco said to give him a call after we met."

Once Mandy was alone, she tried to force her nerves to calm down, but they were still jangled. She never liked surprises like this.

The second line on the phone at the desk was lit up, meaning Tony was still on with Ricco. She was tempted to call Ricco's assistant to ask what was going on, but she refrained. Too many people knowing her insecurities would only make things worse.

Since the next appointment wasn't due for another hour, she busied herself filing cards and organizing the desk. School was in session, and it was too close to lunchtime to expect preschooler walk-ins.

The sound of Tony's voice startled her. "Got a minute for a quick chat?"

"Now?"

He nodded. "Yeah."

Her heart pounded. Here it was, the reason he suddenly appeared without warning. She swallowed hard and nodded. "Here or in the office?"

"Here is fine."

She took the liberty of studying his face as he gathered his thoughts. Thick eyebrows hooded his deep-set dark eyes. His jawline was strong, and his temples pulsed when he wasn't talking.

"So what did you want to discuss?"

He lifted the top sheet from the notepad and pulled out a slip of paper she recognized. The one she'd jotted her to-do list on. And that included—oh no. Her heart sank.

"I see that you were going to apply for the manager's position," he said softly.

Mandy's mouth went dry. She nodded. There was no point in denying she wanted the title and pay to go with what she'd been doing since Parker had left. If she'd known someone else was coming, she wouldn't have left it by the phone in the office.

"I wasn't trying to snoop," he said. "It was right there in front of me."

"That's okay." What else could she have said?

"Sorry."

The straight line of his lips and his sympathetic gaze made her stomach churn. She hated people feeling sorry for her.

"There's something I think you should know about me," he said.

"Really?" Her own sarcasm surprised her. "Sorry, I didn't mean it to sound so. . ."

He smiled sympathetically. "That's okay. This is very awkward, and I understand, but there's a reason I was brought here. You see, I'm—well, Edward is my uncle."

"Edward?" she asked as realization dawned on her. "As in Edward Rossi, founder and president of Small World?"

"Yep, that's the one."

She couldn't think of anything to say.

"I didn't really want this job," he went on, "and I don't expect to be here long, so I'll make sure to put in a good word when they move me back to Atlanta."

"Thanks." She didn't dare say anything else, or she'd risk sounding surly.

As conflicting thoughts continued to collide in her head, Tony jotted down a few things on his pad. She wanted to grab his pencil, break it in two, then snatch the notepad and read what he was writing about her.

He stopped writing and looked directly at her. "If it's any consolation, I've heard you're one of the best photographers in the district."

❧

Tony knew he shouldn't continue standing there staring at

her while she processed what he'd just said. She needed time alone.

"I have a few things to do, so I'll be in the office. If you need me, just holler."

"I'll be fine."

He offered a smile. "I'm sure you will." After he took a few steps toward the office, he stopped, turned, and waited for her to look up. "Mandy, I'm sure someday you'll make an excellent manager. I'm sorry you had to find out this way."

Her lips quivered for a split second before she nodded. She opened her mouth to say something, but all that came out was a squeak.

"If you need some time off, let me know, okay?"

Her face looked stricken. "Why would I need time off?"

"I'm just saying. . ."

"I don't."

She took a step back and slammed into the corner of the wall. Tony instinctively reached for her as she rubbed her shoulder.

"I'm fine," she said softly before glancing at his hand resting on her arm.

He quickly pulled his hand back and shoved it into his pocket. "That's fine. I just wanted to let you know it's okay if you need time to think about things."

There wasn't even the hint of a smile on her pretty face as she stood there staring at him with those wide, long-lash-framed hazel eyes.

Tony didn't want to torture her, so he added, "After I get acclimated to the place, I'll need to start interviewing for another full-time photographer. Since you'll be training the person, I'd like for you to participate."

She didn't say a word, so he took off for the office. This had been much more difficult than he'd anticipated.

He closed the door behind him and hesitated as he looked around the room. Mandy had all but made the space her own.

A trio of butterfly prints adorned one wall, while a collage of portraits, probably from this very studio, hung on the adjacent wall. A small dish of pastel mints rested on the corner of the desk—behind the vase of spring flowers.

His first inclination was to remove some of the feminine touches, but he paused and closed his eyes. *Lord, guide me in how to handle this situation. Mandy is obviously distressed, and rightfully so. I don't want to upset her, but I want to do well with the job I've been hired to do. Oh, and while You're at it, help me work on my attitude about being where I don't want to be.*

two

Christina's flight was two hours late. Mandy had thought to check the flight before leaving to pick her up, but she left early to avoid talking to Tony more than necessary—at least until she had time to process his being there. Why did he have to be so nice and so. . .good-looking? When Mandy arrived at the terminal, she spotted Christina standing between two tall, very attractive men. The only surprise was that Christina was already there—not the fact that she was flanked by guys.

Mandy popped her trunk, and the guys loaded it. "Thanks for everything," Christina said. "I hope your mother gets better soon."

"Thanks, Chrissy, I'm sure she'll be fine," one of the men said.

The other guy looked like he was about to hug her, but when she leaned away from him, he pulled back. "Try to look at the bright side of things. Call me if you need more advice."

"Thanks, guys."

"Nice talking to you, Chrissy."

As soon as Mandy got in the car and snapped her seat belt, she turned to her sister. "Chrissy? I thought you hated people calling you that."

Christina shrugged. "A lot has changed since I left."

Mandy gave her a once-over before starting the car and pulling away from the curb. "You'll have to tell me all about it after I get off work tonight. I'll take you to Mom and Dad's, but I have to run back to the studio."

"Can't you take some time off?" Christina sounded hurt. "Mom says you haven't taken a vacation since you started that job."

"There's been a new development at work, and I'm not sure

15

what's going on," Mandy explained. "I have a new boss."

Christina groaned. "Is this person a jerk, or something?"

"I can't tell yet, but so far, he seems okay."

"Did he get the job you were talking about applying for?"

Mandy nodded. "Yeah, and not only that, his uncle is head of the company."

"Sorry, sis. That's always the way it is, though."

"Okay, what gives?" Mandy asked. "I've never seen you so negative. What happened in LA?"

Christina lifted her hands and dropped them in her lap. "So many things I don't even know where to begin. That place is insane."

"Did you expect anything else?"

"I knew it would be different from here, but I figured once I got to know the right people, things would fall into place."

That's how it has always been for Christina, Mandy thought. Between her sweet disposition and drop-dead gorgeous looks, most people loved her. She was smart, too, but no one ever bothered to take the time to find that out.

"You weren't there long, though," Mandy said softly. "Maybe you just didn't give it enough time." She cut her glance over to Christina who smoothed the side of her skirt.

"I was there long enough to realize that's not what I really want. There's so much more to being an actor than acting."

Mandy chuckled. "It's like that with everything."

"I'm sure it is, but I like it here better, where you can take people at face value and not some image they've created for the public."

"Wanna talk about Joe?" Mandy patted her sister's hand. "I understand if you don't."

"I guess I might as well tell you now," Christina said. "Joe was such a sweet guy at first. He even went to church with me, but then he got offered this really big part, and suddenly I had to take a backseat to his career, and church wasn't important to him anymore. I just never saw it coming."

"Is that why you left LA and came home—just because

some guy dumped you?" The instant the words left Mandy's mouth, she regretted the harshness. "That didn't come out right."

"Nah, that's okay. I know what you're saying. It's not the whole reason, but after all the stuff I went through, it was the final straw."

They'd reached their parents' house. Mandy turned off the car and turned to face her sister. "I have to get back to the studio, and I'm working late tonight, so why don't you relax with Mom and Dad, and we'll get together tomorrow after I get off?"

"Sounds good."

As soon as they had all of Christina's bags in the foyer, Mandy left. All the way back to work, she thought about the parallel between her and Christina's lives. Both had high expectations, and now they faced disappointment due to naïveté.

Mandy found a parking spot close to the studio entrance. She took a few deep breaths before getting out of her car and heading back to work. Fortunately, her appointment hadn't arrived yet, so she had time to get the studio ready before the children came in. She headed to the back with props in one basket and candy in another.

"Are you always this organized?"

She glanced up to see Tony leaning against the studio door frame, one long leg crossed over the other, arms folded, eyes twinkling, and his lips twitching into a grin. So far, with the exception of the fact that he had the job she wanted, there was nothing about this man *not* to like.

"Makes it a lot easier to handle squirmy kids."

"No wonder you're one of the company favorites."

She lifted one eyebrow and looked at him. The fact that he was trying too hard to be nice bugged her. He glanced at her in amusement.

"Maybe you'll want to give me some pointers before I start working with the children."

Mandy paused, hand in midair. "Haven't you worked with children before?"

He shrugged. "Just a few times—but I always had their parents' help. I'd like to be able to do it on my own like you do."

Mandy shook her head. *This was so unfair.*

Then she remembered the sermon from a few weeks ago about how life wasn't fair. She swallowed hard and tried to focus on how much more Jesus had to face than she ever would.

"Will you be able to work with me, Mandy?"

She knew he'd closed some of the distance between them, but she didn't look up. "Yes, of course."

"I believe in open communication, so if there's anything you want to discuss, don't wait until it's too late."

"Too late?" She snapped her gaze to his.

"I don't want you to worry about anything. If you need to discuss something, I want you to let me know right away, instead of assuming things." His empathetic—or was it sympathetic?—expression made her stomach churn. "And now that I'm here, you don't have to take on so much responsibility."

She bristled. "Okay."

Mandy wished Tony would leave her alone to do her work. With him standing there, watching, concentration was difficult.

"Just wanted to make sure." The phone rang. "I'll get that."

After he left, she quickened her pace. She adjusted the last light when Tony appeared at the door.

"Your sister needs to talk to you." He held the cordless phone toward her. "I'll finish up here."

"No need. I'm done." Mandy took the phone and walked toward the hallway leading to the offices and storage area. "I won't be long."

Christina got right to the point. "Mom wants to know if you can come for dinner."

"I don't know."

"She's making chicken fried steak and mashed potatoes and gravy."

Mandy laughed in spite of her frustration. "She sure knows how to lure me in."

"It was my idea," Christina said. "I wanted to make sure you came."

"That's very sweet, but my job—"

"I miss you, Mandy. Please come, do this for me. It'll be like old times."

Old times, where the family sat around the table, Mom at one end and Dad at the other. All the attention would be focused on Christina and whatever she'd been up to lately. Okay, so she was being childish.

"Let me see what I can do. One of the part-timers is scheduled to come in, so I might be able to get away."

"Call and let us know, okay?"

"Sure," Mandy said. "I gotta run. My appointment will be here any minute."

She clicked the button to disconnect and brought the phone to the office to place it back on the cradle. Tony still hadn't changed anything in the room. Even her mints remained untouched.

"Everything okay?" Tony hovered in the doorway, watching her.

She nodded. "My sister wants me to come to my parents' house for dinner. I told her I'd have to get back with her, since it's one of our late nights."

"You should go."

"Bella is scheduled to come in at four thirty, and she's pretty good with the kids."

Tony pursed his lips for a moment before speaking. "I'm perfectly capable of handling clients."

"I didn't say—"

"You and I need to sit down and come to some terms, Mandy. Yes, I understand if you have hard feelings toward me, but we'll be working together—at least until Uncle Ed thinks I'm ready for the home office. If I hadn't taken time out to join the army, I'd be where I want to be right now, but until then—"

"I don't have hard feelings." At least she didn't want to.

A sympathetic grin flashed over his lips. "Good. But we still need to talk. Maybe we can squeeze in some time between appointments."

The electronic buzzer sounded, alerting them that her appointment had arrived. "Sounds good." She took off toward the front and greeted the family. "What a pretty dress, Audrey!"

"My mommy got it for me." The little girl gestured toward her sister. "Anna got a new dress, too."

"Both of you look so nice. Come on into the studio, and we'll get started."

The girls had been to the Small World Portrait Studio before, so they knew the ropes. Mandy waved at their mother, who waved back as she sat down with a magazine. Mandy noticed Tony's eagle eyes, watching, waiting. Her hands shook until she was out of his vision.

"If we're good, do we get candy?" Anna asked.

Mandy tilted her head and nodded. "Absolutely."

Anna giggled and poked Audrey in the side. "Don't make baby faces when she takes our picture. I want candy."

If Tony hadn't made another appearance, Mandy would have commented, but he managed to render her incapable of her normal silly retorts that resulted in giggles from the kids. Instead, she lifted the multicolored toucan from the basket of props. "Say hi to Mr. Toucan."

She snapped the shot at the precise moment both girls grinned. Her next prop was a soft, brown teddy bear.

"Can I hold him?" Audrey asked as she stuck her thumb in her mouth.

Anna yanked on Audrey's hand. "Don't act like a baby, or we won't get any candy."

Fifteen minutes later, Mandy had enough shots for the

girls' mother to choose from. As soon as Mandy was done, Tony lifted the basket of candy and motioned for the girls. Mandy started to tell him to hand them each one piece, but before she had a chance to say a word, they rushed toward him and knocked the basket out of his hand, sending candy flying in every direction.

Anna squealed with delight, and Audrey gathered as much as her tiny hands would hold. Anna pointed to Mandy, who gave them the sternest look she could manage. "Put it back in the basket, Audrey. Miss Mandy only lets us have one."

Audrey pouted but did as her sister told her. "I want two pieces."

Mandy sighed. "Okay, just for being such good girls and helping me pick up all this candy, you may each have two." A couple of minutes later, all the candy was back in the basket and each child had a lollipop with a safety stick. "Give me a few minutes to organize them, and you can see what we have," Mandy said to their mother.

Anna and Audrey sat down at the play center in the corner of the waiting area, while their mother continued to read her magazine. Tony joined Mandy as she organized the pictures on the computer screen.

"You're a gifted photographer," he said softly. "I only have one concern that I didn't think about until after the, um, candy incident."

She paused and turned to face him. "A concern?"

"Was it okay with your manager to bribe kids with candy? What if their parents don't approve?"

"When I suggested giving the kids little rewards, Parker said it would be okay, so we always ask the parents when we book the appointments and note it in their files. Most parents don't mind candy, but if they do, we have other thank-you rewards like stickers or age-appropriate trinkets. A little positive reinforcement can go a long way."

Tony studied her then nodded. "Sounds like you have everything under control." He shook his head and laughed.

"You were good back there. I had no idea what to do."

I have control over everything but my career. "When people pay to get photos of their children, they expect us to do it right. There's such a small window of opportunity."

He lifted his eyebrows. "True."

"Do you have children?" The instant those words left her mouth, she regretted saying them. Tony's personal life wasn't any of her business. But now that she'd brought it up, she wanted to know.

It didn't seem to bother him. "Not yet." After a brief pause, he added, "I'd like to someday, though—when the right person comes along."

"Sorry, it's none of my business." She cast her glance downward.

"That's okay, Mandy. We'll be working closely, and I don't mind if you ask personal questions."

He obviously hadn't read the same manual as Parker, the former manager, who felt that work should be all business and personal lives should remain at home. That had taken some getting used to, but she'd adapted and appreciated it after he quit. Not knowing much about the man had been a blessing when she didn't feel anything but the combination of annoyance that he'd left without warning and relief he was gone.

After she had all the pictures arranged and the girls' mother had chosen those she wanted made into prints, Tony encouraged Mandy to call her sister back and accept the dinner invitation. "After I get back to Atlanta, you better believe I won't turn down a good meal," he said with a smile.

Maybe she should stay at the studio and send Tony to her parents' house instead. The thought flickered through her mind so quickly she caught herself smiling.

"I'm glad I made you smile," he said. "Now go on and have fun with your family. We'll be fine here."

She nodded then looked pointedly at her watch. "It's not time yet."

"Committed to your job." He paused and looked at her. "Every manager's dream."

She didn't want to be the manager's dream; she wanted to be the manager. All kinds of sarcastic thoughts darted around in her mind, but she knew enough to keep them to herself.

Christina answered the phone when Mandy called to accept the dinner invitation. "I am so excited! It'll be like old times."

"Yeah. Old times."

She'd barely hung up the phone when Tony walked up. "Everything okay?" The look on his face was one of concern.

"Sure." She smoothed the sides of her pants. "Thanks for giving me some time off this evening."

"It's not exactly time off," he reminded her. "You've already worked more than forty hours this week. I don't want you getting burned out."

"I don't think my work is suffering."

"That's not what I'm saying." His instant seriousness disarmed her.

Mandy had to clear her throat. "I've always been committed to my job," she said softly. "I don't mind working long hours." She left out the fact that she didn't have anything or anyone to go home to.

He chewed on his bottom lip for a few seconds. "That's going to change. From now on, you'll only work forty hours. If my uncle or cousin saw you were still working long hours, they would be upset with both of us."

"I understand."

He looked at her then nodded.

She would have preferred his job—not fewer hours. "I have work to do." She turned around and walked away, leaving him standing there alone. It took the rest of the time in the studio to calm down, and when it was time to leave, she stuck her head in his office. "I'm going now."

He narrowed his eyes and nodded without saying a word. That was just fine with Mandy.

When she got to her parents' house, she was annoyed even more that their mother was treating Christina like a child. Occasionally, Mandy caught Christina studying her as if seeing her for the first time.

"What?" Mandy finally asked.

Christina tilted her head and pouted. "You're mad at me, aren't you?"

"No." Mandy realized she was taking her frustrations out on her sister. "It's just that work, well—"

"You work entirely too many hours. You need to get out and have some fun." Their mother looked at Christina. "Perhaps the two of you can find something interesting to do."

"Sounds good to me," Christina said.

"Now that we have a new manager, I'll have more time. He's trying to cut back on overtime."

"You have a new man in your office?" Their mother leaned forward and grinned. "Is he single?"

"Mo—*om*," Mandy groaned. "He's my boss. That's it."

"You never know," Mom said. "Lots of women meet their future husbands at the office."

Maybe so, but Mandy would be willing to bet those future husbands didn't steal the jobs those women wanted. "Let's just drop this, okay?"

After dinner, Mandy automatically started clearing the table. Christina was about to go into the living room, until she locked gazes with Mandy. She pursed her lips then lifted some dishes and followed Mandy into the kitchen.

"You don't have to do that," their mother said. "You just got home."

Mandy held her breath, waiting for Christina to put everything down. To her surprise, Christina shook her head. "I don't want Mandy stuck with the cleanup. It'll go faster if I help." She made a shooing gesture. "Why don't you go hang out with Dad while Mandy and I load the dishwasher?"

After their mother left, Christina turned to Mandy. "Now I get why you always acted the way you did."

Mandy had been about to stick the flatware in the tray. She stopped and looked at Christina. "What are you talking about?"

Christina frowned. "I always thought you were jealous of me."

three

"You're kidding, right?" Mandy glared at Christina then rolled her eyes. "I don't think so."

Christina persisted. "Mom and Dad don't expect as much from me as they do you."

"Why would that make me jealous?"

"That's what I want to know," Christina said. "I always wished I could be as smart as you."

"So while you thought I was jealous of you, you were actually jealous of me?"

Christina made a face. "Something like that. Weird, huh?"

Mandy shrugged. "I dunno. Sibling relationships can be complicated, I suppose."

"I want you to know how much I appreciate you."

That simple comment caused a lump to form in Mandy's throat. She swallowed hard. "Thank you."

"I mean it. When we were little, you always made sure people were nice to me. Then when I started high school, you and your friends were so helpful."

"We didn't exactly travel in the same circles," Mandy reminded her. "Your friends were a lot cooler than mine."

"But yours were smarter, and look at them now."

Mandy cast a comical glance at Christina. "Uh-huh, right. Ya know, there were times I would have traded smart for pretty."

"You're just as pretty, but you never noticed." Christina shrugged. "But that's not the point. I had the best of both worlds—my circle of friends and yours."

Mandy bobbed her head. "True."

Christina gave Mandy a playful shove. "You don't have to be so agreeable."

Mandy smiled and picked up a towel. "If we don't agree, you know who'll win." She winked and pointed her thumb to her chest. "*Moi*."

Silence fell between them as they finished doing the dishes. Mandy was about to say good-bye when Christina's eyes lit up.

"Hey, I have an idea! Why don't you spend the night?"

"I have to work tomorrow," Mandy said. "Maybe some other time, and I'll bring my stuff."

"Small World doesn't even open until ten. You can go home in the morning to get ready for work. Mom always keeps extra toothbrushes."

"I don't know."

Christina tilted her head and gave Mandy one of her irresistible puppy-dog looks. "Please?"

Mandy laughed. "You still have it, baby sister. Okay, I'll stay."

Christina didn't bother trying to hide her joy. She pumped her fist, grinning. "I knew you couldn't say no. Let's watch one of our old movies. I'll get Mom to make popcorn, and we can have a party."

Mandy tilted her head forward. "I think we're perfectly capable of making our own popcorn. Let's show Mom how grown up you can be."

"Sorry. It's so easy to fall back into old habits around Mom and Dad."

"Especially since they still want to baby you." Mandy was proud of Christina for acknowledging the truth. "Are you planning to stick around and get a job here in Wheeling?"

"Looks like I don't have a choice," Christina admitted. "I obviously don't have what it takes to be an actor. I thought all I'd have to do was go into an audition, say a few lines, and walk around the stage. It's a lot harder than it looks." She crinkled her nose. "Plus they want actors to do all kinds of other stuff that's totally not fun, like talk shows and interviews and stuff."

"I understand."

Christina leaned against the kitchen counter and looked down at the floor, shaking her head. "I have no idea what I want to do now, though. All I ever wanted was to be an actress."

Mandy gave her sister a sympathetic pat on the shoulder. "I know, sweetie, but things don't always turn out like we expect. I'm going through my own disappointment now, and it's not fun. I always thought I'd be in a high-level management position that commanded respect, but instead, I'm working for the boss's nephew." She got in her sister's line of view. "We'll get through this. Let's go find a movie."

❧

Tony arrived at the studio an hour before they opened. He expected Mandy to be there, or at least follow soon after. She was such a dedicated employee, he started to worry when he looked at the clock fifteen minutes before opening time, and she still hadn't arrived.

As he worked on getting the front ready for customers, he thought about how good Mandy was with the children. He even caught himself thinking what a good mother she'd be someday, then he quickly forced those inappropriate thoughts from his mind.

Every few minutes, he opened the front door to look down the street, but still no Mandy. He checked the phone messages, and there was nothing from her. Just as he was about to look up her number, he saw her approach the door.

Her short blond hair glistened as she walked in and glided across the floor. He loved the flicker of acknowledgment in her hazel eyes when she glanced in his direction. Tony couldn't ignore the fact that he was immensely attracted to Mandy Pruitt.

"Sorry I'm late," she said. "I stayed at my parents' house, so I had to go home and get ready for work this morning."

"You're not late."

"I like to get here early to prepare."

"Everything's all done." He glanced at his watch and nodded toward the back. "Why don't you go put your stuff in the office, and I'll open?"

As soon as she walked to the back, Tony relaxed his shoulders. *Lord, please don't let me step over the line with Mandy.*

❧

An awkward silence fell between them. At ten thirty, the phone rang.

"Mandy," Christina said, "Mom says Dad wants me to get a job right away, but I have no idea where to start looking."

"Why don't you call some of your old friends and see if they know of any job openings?" Mandy rested the phone on her shoulder while she slipped the envelope from the last client into the file slot.

"They all work in boring office jobs. I want something fun."

"Then why don't you try some of the shops in town? You like fashion."

"I don't know," Christina said.

"You'll even get a discount."

"I'll think about it."

A shadow at the doorway drew Mandy's attention. She glanced up to see Tony leaning against the door frame, watching her. "I gotta go. I'll call you later." She pressed the END button on the phone and looked him directly in the eye. "Did you need something?"

"What time is your first appointment?"

"Eleven. Why?"

"Just checking. What do you normally do between appointments?"

Why was he grilling her? She bristled at the very thought of having someone standing over her, expecting the worst, since every minute of time she'd spent at the studio was focused on work—at least it was until her sister came back to town.

"I do follow-up and make calls," she replied. "Did you have something else you wanted me to do?"

He shook his head as he pulled away from where he'd been

leaning. "You're doing everything right. In fact, the folks in the home office are impressed by how well this location has done without a manager."

Then why did they send Tony? She kept her thoughts to herself. "I follow the guidelines from my training."

"That's another thing," he said. "We're in the process of overhauling the training program. Apparently, some of the managers think it has some antiquated concepts."

Mandy thought for a moment. "I think it can use some updating, but the basic concepts are good." She shrugged. "At least they work for me."

Tony glanced at his watch. "I need to let you go get ready for your appointment. We can discuss this later. If you have some suggestions, I'm sure Edward and Ricco would appreciate input from a *successful* employee."

As Mandy prepared the studio for her next appointment, she thought about Tony's comments. If she'd been such a successful employee, as he'd put it, why had they brought him here? She slammed the basket of props on the tiny table next to the camera, sending a few skittering over the edge and across the floor, then instantly regretted it. Not getting to even apply for the promotion didn't justify bad behavior—and she certainly didn't need to let Tony see her acting out.

"Drop something?" When she glanced up, she saw Tony standing six feet away, holding one of the stuffed animals from the basket.

Lord, please work on my attitude and spirit. You know what I need and what I should have. I need to trust You more with my future.

He gestured over his shoulder. "Your appointment's here."

She took a deep breath and slowly let it out. She needed to maintain a positive attitude for her clients—especially since these were some of the most difficult toddlers she'd ever worked with.

It took several attempts to get the children to calm down, but Mandy finally managed to capture some cute poses.

Their mother was frantic as she crossed the studio floor and took the hands of her three- and four-year-old. "I'm so sorry they can't sit still. I do everything the doctor says, including not let them have sugar, but they won't stop wiggling."

Mandy sympathized with the young mother. "Maybe they'll grow up to become athletes."

The woman looked at both of her children then offered a grateful look to Mandy. "That would be nice."

She heard Tony's footsteps as he entered the studio. "You have a visitor," he said. "It's your sister."

"Thanks, I'll be there in a few minutes."

"I can take over," he offered. Mandy looked him in the eye, and they both smiled. "Maybe not." Still grinning, he headed for the door.

After he left, the children's mother ushered her kids toward the front. "I'll take them for a little walk while you get the computer proofs ready."

"Thanks. Come back in half an hour, and I'll have them done."

After they left, Mandy straightened up for the next session before going to see what Christina wanted. When she arrived in the lobby, she was surprised to see Christina and Tony engrossed in a conversation about her parents. "You wouldn't believe how good our mother's cooking is. Maybe you can come for dinner sometime."

Mandy cringed. She needed to get her sister out of there— and fast!

Tony offered Mandy an amused look and winked. "I just might. That is, if Mandy doesn't mind."

Christina looked at Mandy, clasped her hands, and put them beneath her chin. "Can you go have coffee with me?"

"I don't normally take a break," Mandy said. "What's up?"

"It's okay if you need to take a break," Tony offered. "I can show the proofs."

"No," Mandy said. "I'd like to do that."

Tony winked at Mandy then turned to Christina. "After a

little fiasco with a basket of candy and a couple of starving kids, she doesn't trust me here alone."

"That's not—"

She stopped when she noticed the smirk on Tony's face.

"Why don't I go to that cute little boutique on the corner, and I'll come back for you later?" Christina said.

"Can you give me about an hour?"

"Um. . .sure."

After Christina left, Mandy quickly organized the proofs on the computer screen. The children and their mother arrived shortly afterward.

"I like all of them," the young mother said. "You're the only photographer who's been able to make them look like normal kids rather than little monsters."

"Monster!" As soon as he hollered the word, the four-year-old lifted his hands with bent fingers to look like claws, and he started chasing his little sister around the waiting area.

The mother rolled her eyes. "Why don't we just go with the first three? I'd like the economy package."

Mandy smiled. "Sounds great."

Tony cleared his throat, but Mandy forced herself to ignore him. She knew he was trying to get her to upsell the customer—something the company put high on their list of priorities.

Once the mom and her children left, Mandy finished the order then turned to Tony. "I never try to upsell her because they come in every three months and get the economy package. She can barely afford that."

"You don't even try?" he asked.

"I did once, and I thought she might break down and cry when she had to tell me they couldn't afford what she really wanted."

Tony pursed his lips. By the time he finally nodded his agreement, she was ready to argue. "You did the right thing. There is a line we shouldn't cross at the risk of losing good customers." He gestured toward the door. "Your sister's back.

Why don't you go for coffee?"

Christina stood by the door twirling her bright yellow handbag. Mandy blinked. She'd had a tan one earlier.

"C'mon, I can't take too long."

"Don't look now, but that guy from the electronics store across the street is staring at us," Christina said.

Mandy groaned. "That's Brent. He gets these crushes on people, and it's my turn."

Christina giggled. "He's cute in a geeky sort of way."

"Yeah, he's not bad-looking, and he's pretty nice, but he can be annoying."

As they got farther away from the studio and the electronics store, Mandy pointed to the bag. "New purse?"

"Yes, isn't it cute?" Christina held it up for Mandy to get a better look. "I saw it in the store window, and I had to have it." She held it up for Mandy to touch. "Feel it."

Mandy gently slid her hand over the soft, pebbled leather. "Very nice. Feels like real leather."

"Lambskin."

"I thought you were broke."

"Dad gave me some money."

"He did?" Mandy asked. An odd feeling swept over her—a blend of shock and sibling rivalry. "To go shopping? Does he know what you're doing with the money?"

Christina slowly shook her head. "Please don't say anything."

"How about reimbursing me for the plane ticket? You said you were going to."

"Um. . .I'll do that after I get all settled." Christina gave Mandy a sheepish look. "Dad said it was to get me through until I found a job."

"I don't think he intended for you to go on a shopping spree." As they approached the coffee shop, Mandy dug her wallet out of her modest bag. "I'll treat this time. Just please don't keep spending his money on things you don't absolutely have to have."

The instant they sat down, Christina's eyes lit up. "Why didn't you tell me your new boss was so cute?"

"He's my *boss*. I don't think of him that way."

Christina rolled her eyes. "C'mon, we're sisters. You're not blind."

"I really don't want to talk about my boss."

"That's just silly," Christina said. "If he were my boss—"

"He's not your boss, so don't worry about it," Mandy interrupted.

For the next fifteen minutes, Christina talked about how she'd called all her old friends, and they didn't have time to talk because they were so busy. "I can't believe no one has time for me anymore."

"Work has a way of doing that to people," Mandy said. "Did you ask anyone if they knew of a job?"

"No. I don't think any of their jobs sound like fun."

"While you were shopping, did you ask if they had openings?"

Christina frowned. "Not yet. Why are you grilling me so hard?"

"Because I think Mom and Dad are right. It's time for you to get a job."

"Okay, okay." Christina held up her hands. "I didn't expect you to be so grouchy."

Mandy glanced at her watch. "I need to get back to the studio now. While you're here, why don't you walk around and see if you can fill out at least one application for work? There are so many businesses, one of them is bound to be hiring."

Still frowning, Christina nodded. "All right. I'll try, but there aren't that many jobs out there."

"Just ask. That's all I'm saying. If you keep trying, you'll eventually get a job."

When they got back to Small World, Tony glanced up. "Did you two have fun?"

"A blast," Mandy said sarcastically.

Tony blinked in confusion before turning to Christina. "It

was nice meeting you."

"Same here," she said. "Um, Mandy, I don't have anything to wear to church, and Mom said she wants me to go with you."

"How about all those clothes in your overstuffed suitcases?"

Christina flicked her hand from the wrist. "Those are LA clothes. Mom says they're not appropriate for church here."

Since Christina was a good four inches taller and at least two sizes smaller, Mandy couldn't very well offer to lend her one of her dresses. "Why don't you use some of Dad's money to get a new outfit? I'm sure he wouldn't mind."

Christina glanced down at her shoes—which probably cost more than Mandy's entire outfit—before looking back. "I used it all on the purse—and these shoes."

Rather than cause a scene in front of her boss, she pulled some money from her own bag and thrust it at her sister. "You can pay me back when you get a job."

"Thanks." Christina looked at the wad of money then frowned. "I'll have to find something on sale." She paused then broke into a grin. "It'll be fun—sort of like an Easter egg hunt."

Mandy was embarrassed that this happened in front of Tony, but it was too late. After Christina left, she turned to Tony.

"Sorry about that. My sister is very sweet, but being the baby, Mom, Dad, and I gave in to her a lot."

He chuckled. "I understand. I have a baby sister, too."

"We have three sessions scheduled for this afternoon, so I'll get the studio ready."

"Before you do that, Mandy, I have a question."

She stopped and turned to face him. "Okay."

He rubbed his chin and studied the floor. "Your sister mentioned going to church with you." He looked up and directly into her eyes. "I've been looking for a church home. Where do you go?"

four

Mandy was caught off guard. It never dawned on her that Tony might be a Christian.

"It's okay if you don't want to tell me," he said. "I understand if you don't want me to go to your church."

She felt terrible. "No, I'm okay with it." She reached for a slip of paper and jotted down the church address. "We have Sunday services at nine and eleven, with Bible classes in between."

He took the paper, looked at it for a few seconds, then met her gaze. "Thanks, Mandy. I'll be there on Sunday morning, probably first service."

"That's when I go," she said. "I've always been sort of an early bird."

"Me, too."

As soon as Mandy got to the camera area, she felt like kicking herself. What did he care if she was an early bird? He wasn't her friend; he was her boss.

❧

Tony loved that Mandy was a Christian. Even though Small World was founded and owned by Christians, they didn't limit themselves in who they hired, as long as the applicant's references and backgrounds checked out. Their philosophy was to be a shining example from management on down, knowing Christ would do all the work to win hearts.

❧

Mandy had had back-to-back appointments until late afternoon, when Tony joined her at the camera. "Bella just called in sick," he said.

"She was supposed to close tonight."

"I know. She also had an appointment scheduled right

when you were supposed to leave."

Inwardly groaning, Mandy thought about how exhausted she was. But she didn't want to let on to Tony, so she squared her shoulders. "That's fine. I don't mind closing."

He shook his head. "Let's split the responsibility. If you don't mind taking her client while I go grab a quick bite at the deli, I'll close."

"But—"

"You're not in this alone anymore, Mandy," he said firmly.

Mandy's gaze locked with Tony's. His kindness filled her with warmth. She quickly looked away. "Okay, that's fine."

Tony waited around until her appointment arrived, then he left with a wave. "I'll get my food and bring it back here," he said.

"You don't have to—" His expression stopped her, mid-sentence. "Okay."

Once again, he held her gaze a couple of seconds longer than necessary, causing her insides to feel as though they were plummeting to the floor. She looked away to regain her focus.

As difficult as it was to admit, he'd been kind and fair from the moment they first met—even though he did seem a bit grouchy at first. If he'd been a dictatorial jerk, it would have been easier to justify being angry at the company.

The buzzer on the door sounded, alerting her to the next client appointment. After she assured the parents everything would be okay, and letting them know they could even watch from the door, she began positioning the children for their photos. Her notes stated that they weren't allowed candy, so she pulled out some of the more colorful props to get their attention. It took her forty-five minutes to get a half-dozen good shots.

After she finished, she ushered the children back to their waiting parents. "Give me a half hour to put this together, and you can choose the package you like," she said.

The father looked pleased. "Last time we had studio

portraits done, we had to wait weeks for the proofs."

His wife laughed. "I forgot to tell my husband this is all high-tech now."

Mandy grinned. "You'll have the finished package in just a few days."

"That's wonderful," the children's father said. He slapped one of the company brochures on his palm. "And from what I've seen of your prices, we can come here often as the kids grow up."

She heard a rustling sound from the office down the hall, letting her know that Tony had slipped back into the studio sometime while she was photographing the children. After the family left, he joined her.

"Why don't you head on out now, Mandy? I'll stick around until closing."

"Are you okay with walk-ins?" The instant those words left her mouth, she remembered she wasn't in charge. He was the manager, not her, and if he wasn't okay, he'd have to deal with the consequences.

He didn't seem fazed. "I'm fine. Remember, they put me through the crash course. I'm sure I'm not as good as you, but I don't think anyone is." He grinned and winked. "At least now I know what to do if some kid gets out of control and sends candy flying. Your family is waiting."

Mandy smiled. "If things get crazy, call, okay?" She grabbed her purse and made a beeline for the door, where she stopped, turned, and faced Tony, who stood behind the counter, head down, focused on some of the reply cards from their last mailing.

When he glanced up, the look of consternation on his face touched her heart. "Need something?" he asked.

"No, I'm fine. I just wanted to. . ." She licked her lips and smiled. "I wanted to thank you for being so understanding." Then she ran out the door before he had a chance to say a word.

She was at her parents' house in just a few minutes, and her mother pointed to the table. "Set a place for yourself, dear."

Dinnertime conversation centered on Christina's lack of a job, which was typical, but now it suited Mandy just fine. However, right before dessert, her father put down his fork and leaned toward Mandy. "Have you discussed that promotion with the company executives?" he asked.

Mandy had been perfectly content not being in the limelight, but with such a direct question, she had to answer. "No, but that's a moot point now. They put a family member in charge."

"They might not have known you were interested," he said. "Did you ever tell anyone?"

"Well, yes, but I was told to apply as soon as they posted the position." She squirmed in her chair. "They never posted it."

"Mandy, hon, I know you like to play by the rules, but sometimes the rules don't apply."

Christina had been quiet, but now she nodded her agreement. "Yeah, you really do need to let people know you're not a doormat. Show them what you're made of. Maybe if you dressed a little nicer—"

"Christina," their father said with a warning tone. "You're not exactly the voice of authority on gainful employment."

"But—"

Their dad cut Christina off. "I think your sister knows better than you do."

"It would definitely help if she had clothes that didn't make her invisible," Christina said.

"Stay out. . . ," Mandy said before glancing down at her plate. This was exactly what she dreaded.

"Okay," Christina said, holding up her hands. "But at least you can step up the wardrobe a bit."

Their mother grinned. "I think Mandy looks professional."

"Professional—yes," Christina agreed. "But boring. What's wrong with adding a splash of color here and there, or carrying a great handbag to let people know she's important?"

Mandy shook her head. "I don't need a handbag that costs

more than most people's mortgage to feel important."

Christina shrugged. "Maybe not, but you definitely need something." She smiled at Mandy. "Next time you go shopping, take me with you, and I'll get you out of your rut."

"I think you need to let your supervisor know that you'd like to move up with the company," their dad said, ignoring Christina. "It's his job to relay that information and make sure you have all the tools you need."

Mandy nodded to close the conversation. "Okay, I'll do that."

After she finished helping clear the table, Mandy gave her mother a hug. "Thanks for the food. I really need to go home now."

Her mother followed her to the door and gave her a pleading look. "Please, Mandy? Help your sister—for the family. Christina will be much happier in the long run if she has a good job with her own paycheck."

Mandy couldn't argue. "Okay. Just give me a day or two to think about what I can do."

Before her mother had a chance to say anything else, Mandy took off. All the way to her apartment, she thought about how to help her sister.

Even though Mandy and Christina had the same basic features and people could tell they were sisters, there was a huge difference between them. Christina's blond hair was brighter, and she wore it long, to the middle of her back, while Mandy kept hers cut short to keep it out of her face. They had the same shape of eyes, but Christina framed her blue eyes with black eyeliner and mascara, while Mandy barely swiped her eyelashes with a stroke or two of brown mascara to complement her hazel eyes.

Once she reached her apartment, she locked the door, kicked off her shoes, and flopped onto the sofa. Then she turned on the lamp and picked up the book she'd been reading. As her eyelids drooped, she allowed herself to fall asleep right where she was. The next morning, she awoke with a crick in her neck and her rumpled top twisted around her torso.

With three hours to get ready, Mandy decided to take a long shower and spend a little more time on her makeup. Christina had given her one of the free makeup bags last time she'd been to the cosmetics counter, so she had a trial tube of black mascara and some shiny, tinted lip gloss. The image that stared back from the mirror was in stark contrast to her usual plain look.

Mandy was tempted to wash it all off and start over. She reached for her washrag then stopped. No, she'd keep her clown face on for the day. The children wouldn't care, and the only other people who'd see her were their parents and Tony. The parents were always so frazzled, so she didn't worry about them. Tony, on the other hand. . .

Okay, the last thing she needed to worry about was Tony. Even if he thought she looked ridiculous, so what? She wasn't trying to impress him.

Next, she went to her closet and inspected the contents. Three pairs of black pants, a brown pair, and a couple of khakis were on the left side. She had three skirts—a black pencil skirt, a muted floral tulip skirt, and a brown A-line. Her tops were equally boring, with mostly neutral colors and basic styling. Even the way she organized her closet was boring, with groupings of sleeveless, short-sleeved, and long-sleeved lined up in order of light to dark—white, tan, brown, and black being the predominant colors. On a whim, she'd bought a red cardigan, but the tags still hung from the sleeve, and it was shoved all the way to the end of the rack.

She reached for her typical black slacks and white top. Then, after only a slight hesitation, she grabbed the red cardigan and yanked off the tags. It was time to step outside her narrow box and take chances.

Mandy got in her car and drove to the studio. As she came to a traffic light, she glanced in the mirror over her visor and shook her head. She felt silly about fretting over her makeup and wardrobe.

Shop lights along the street were still dim when she arrived, since most of the businesses hadn't opened yet. A few groups of seniors sat at the tables outside the coffee shop down the street, chatting and enjoying each other's company. Mandy scurried past them, head down, hoping none of the familiar ones would notice her. She was glad when no one called out to her.

She slipped inside the studio and went through her normal routine of putting her purse in the office and setting up for their first customers. The sound of shuffling papers in the manager's office alerted her that Tony was in, but she didn't want to face him-yet.

Five minutes before opening time, Tony appeared on the other side of the counter from where she stood. He stared at her for several seconds before she looked up.

His eyebrows shot up. "You look very nice, Mandy."

"Thank you." Her voice squeaked, so she cleared her throat.

"Is something special going on today that I need to know about?"

"No."

"Red is a good color for you," he continued.

Mandy didn't know what else to say, so she repeated her thanks and changed the subject. "We have several appointments today, and both studios are booked after Bella gets here."

"Oh, Bella called in. She's still sick, and I have to leave for a meeting at the regional office." He offered a smile. "But I called and left a message for Steve to come in."

Mandy nodded. "Good. Thanks."

"We need to hire someone else. I don't know how you've held up as well as you have, but this isn't a good situation."

The phone rang. It was Steve calling to say he couldn't come in because he was studying for finals.

Mandy looked over the schedule and figured out a way to handle all the clients. She only had to call one and reschedule, and they agreed without any problem.

After her first appointment left, Tony handed her a slip of paper with the message, *Your mom called, and she'd like you to call ASAP.*

Mandy took it and went to the smaller of the two offices. Her mother answered after the first ring.

"I'm sending Christina over to see you."

"That's fine, but not now. This isn't a good time," Mandy said. "Today's schedule is crazy. I have to work late and handle an extra load."

"You really need to help us out on this. Your father is upset that she's not out looking for a job, and I told him I'd have you talk to her during your lunch break. She listens to you."

Mandy felt the weight of the world on her shoulders as her mother explained what she wanted her to do. Finally, she agreed and hung up.

Tony appeared at the doorway right when she was leaving. His expression turned to one of concern. "You okay?"

"I'm fine. My sister is having a hard time finding a job, and my mom wants me to talk to her during lunch."

He grinned. "I think it's good that you and your sister are close like that. Why don't you take an extra hour for lunch, since I'll be here, and you'll have to handle everything by yourself tonight?"

"Thanks."

Mandy had one more photo shoot before lunchtime. When she finished, she went out to the front in time to see her sister standing at the counter, with Tony grinning.

five

Mandy turned to Tony. "You did say I could take extra time, right?"

"Absolutely. In fact, if you need even more time, I'll be here until three."

Christina's eyes lit up. "Maybe we can get in a little shopping."

Mandy glanced back and forth between Christina and Tony. "No shopping, Christina. An extra hour is plenty."

Once they were out the door, Christina glanced toward the electronics store. "Where's that cute guy?"

"If you're talking about Brent, he's there somewhere, probably waiting on a customer."

"Maybe I'll go there later and let him wait on me."

"Christina. That's an electronics store."

"What are you saying?"

"You're not exactly a technical genius."

"I can buy electronics as well as the next person."

Based on Mandy's experience with her sister, there was no doubt she could buy *anything* as well as the next person. "I'm sure you can—if you have the money."

"Your boss is *so* cute!" Christina stopped and turned Mandy to face her. "Don't tell me you haven't noticed his cuteness."

Mandy shrugged but wouldn't meet her sister's eye. "He's okay, I guess."

"Okay?" Christina snickered. "Girl, you need some serious man-finding lessons."

"I'm not looking for a man."

"Oh, come on. Don't give me that. You used to tell me that you wanted a traditional marriage, with kids, a house, and"— Christina waved her arms—"the whole kit and caboodle."

"One of these days, yeah."

44

"One of these days is here, Mandy. Open your eyes. You'll be thirty in a couple of years, and the man of your dreams just might be standing in front of you every day."

"Tony's my boss. He doesn't count."

"Sure he counts." Christina grunted. "He's cute and nice. He's probably a Christian, since he asked about churches."

"Yeah, well. . ."

"Don't let a good one get away without at least exploring the possibilities."

Mandy shook her head. "I can't risk losing my job."

"You won't lose your job. He values you too much."

"I don't know about that. He seems annoyed."

"That's because he wanted his family to give him a better job."

Had he actually told her that? She thought of the chatty men at the airport. Mandy let the comment slide. "How am I supposed to, um. . .as you put it, explore possibilities without making a fool of myself?"

"Just keep your eyes open for opportunities to let him know you're interested."

Easy for Christina—guy magnet from way back—to say. "Nah, I'm not interested."

Ignoring her, Christina started making plans. "First, we need to get you some decent clothes."

"What's wrong with my clothes?"

Christina tilted her head and gave her a you're-kidding look. "I've already told you. Bo–ring."

"I'm wearing a red cardigan." Mandy lifted her head slightly as she pulled the sweater together in front.

"*And* black mascara *and* shiny lipstick." Christina nudged her and smiled. "Yes, I noticed."

During lunch, Mandy managed to turn the conversation back to Christina's job hunt. "Did you revamp your résumé to fill in some of those gaps I mentioned?"

Christina nodded. "Yes, and I included the volunteer work you reminded me of. Who would've thought to do that?"

"That's work, and it shows that you didn't just sit around all that time," Mandy said. "And it shows that you care about others."

"True." Christina tapped her finger on her chin. "I'm just not sure where to start."

"How about the places where you love to shop?" Mandy said.

"I'm not so sure about mixing business with pleasure."

Mandy couldn't help but laugh. "There's nothing wrong with selling what you love."

Christina's eyes lit up, and a wide smile broadened her face. "I'll start with that electronics store!"

"You might want to—"

"It's perfect, Mandy! I'll walk up to that cute, geeky guy and ask if he's the manager."

"But he's—"

Christina held up her hand. "Don't tell me anything about him. I don't want to lie."

Mandy settled back in her chair. She might as well accept Christina's scheme, so she smiled back. "Okay, so start there, but don't limit yourself."

"Oh, trust me, I won't." A smile played on Christina's lips. "Ideas are popping into my head all over the place. This job search thing might be fun."

"Whatever you're up to, remember that your main goal is to find employment." Mandy paused and gave her sister a serious look. "Not a man."

"Well, that's all fine and good, but if the Lord gives me an opportunity to meet a man, who am I to turn Him down?"

"Since you put it that way, you're right." Mandy opened her hand. "Mind if I take a look at your new résumé?"

Christina opened the envelope and pulled out a stark white sheet of paper with bulleted lists, just as Mandy had told her to do. "I still don't understand why I shouldn't use fragranced pink paper."

Mandy studied the new résumé and was impressed. "Very

nice. You did everything I recommended."

"I'm not stupid," Christina said. "I might be better than you with fashion, but you have it all over me in the business department."

"If you keep this up"—Mandy thumped the paper—"you'll be a business whiz, too."

Christina's eyes crinkled as she grinned. "Thanks, sis."

Mandy knew the Lord was working in their lives, but she wasn't sure what He was doing. She watched Christina put the résumé back in the folder. As flighty as her sister seemed, there actually was some depth to her. The biggest problem was that no one ever expected much from her. Or maybe that was a good thing.

৯৯

Tony heard the buzzer on the door, so he hopped out of his chair and left the manager's office. It was Brent, the guy he'd met the day before when he stopped by the electronics store across the street for a new phone charger.

"Hey! How's the new job?" Brent asked.

"It's going great." Tony leaned against the counter. "What can I help you with?"

Brent pointed toward the street. "Who was that hot-looking girl I saw Mandy leave with?"

"Her sister, Christina," Tony replied. "I thought you were interested in Mandy."

"I was, but now that I've seen her sister, I think I'm in love."

"With Christina?"

Brent snickered. "Yeah. Think you can arrange for us to meet?"

Tony barely knew Brent, and he was fairly certain that Christina was a Christian. He didn't want to participate in anything that might backfire. "Why don't you talk to Mandy?"

"That would be weird. I've been trying to get a date with her for months, so she might not understand."

"Yeah, that could be awkward." Tony fought the urge to

ask Brent why he'd change his mind, since Mandy was just as pretty and obviously an amazing woman. He spotted the sisters slowing down in front of the electronics store. Mandy said something then waved as Christina entered the store.

"Don't look now, but I think you have a customer."

"That's okay. Matt's there."

"So is Christina," Tony said. "And Mandy's on her way here."

Brent shuffled around in time to face Mandy as she entered the studio. "Hi there, gorgeous!"

Mandy's face reddened. "Uh, hi, Brent."

"Gotta run," he said. "Can't keep the customers waiting."

After he left, Tony pondered how much to tell Mandy. He figured it wouldn't hurt to lay it all on the line. "Brent came here to ask about Christina. He wants to meet her."

Mandy smiled. "Christina thinks he's cute, so this should be interesting."

"Not to be nosy, but what do you know about Brent? Do you think he's a decent guy?"

"I think so—just a little unpolished and slightly annoying, maybe, but he's sweet and harmless."

"Good. I wouldn't want Christina to get herself in a bad position with someone."

Mandy tilted her head and gave him an odd look he couldn't decipher. "Why would you be so concerned about my sister?"

Tony couldn't answer that—even to himself. He was the manager of Small World, not a bodyguard. He couldn't let on how he felt about Mandy so quickly, or she'd think he was taking advantage of his position.

"I just like to see men respect women, that's all," he said.

She narrowed her gaze to study him, then she nodded. "Okay, sounds honorable. I need to set up for the next appointment." With that, she disappeared around the wall separating the lobby from the back, leaving him alone, pondering what was happening.

From the moment he first laid eyes on Mandy Pruitt, he couldn't help but notice the combination of beauty, grace, professionalism—and skepticism toward him, which he found intriguing. Some of the resentment for having to take a job at studio level subsided as he got to know Mandy. The reaction to Christina's presence by Brent and a couple of other men who worked in surrounding stores had amazed him. They were all in awe of Christina, overlooking the sister Tony found more attractive.

Tony shook himself. He needed a swift kick to the backside for even thinking thoughts like that. Mandy was his employee, and he had no business thinking of her in such an unprofessional way.

He had to leave soon, so he made sure Mandy had what she needed. She barely glanced at him when she nodded.

"You know I'll be fine."

"Sorry if I insulted you."

"You didn't."

Except his heart that wouldn't slow down when she met his gaze. He looked away. "Good. I'll have my cell phone on vibrate, so if you need me—"

"I doubt if I'll need you. Go on, or you'll be late."

Rather than argue anymore, he took off toward the parking lot. He'd barely gotten past the electronics store when he heard his name. He spun around to see Christina running to catch up.

"Did you meet Brent?" he asked.

She tossed her hair over one shoulder. "Yes. So how's everything going back at Small World?"

"Great. Your sister is a dynamo at running the place single-handedly."

"She has experience." Her tone instantly changed.

"Does she. . ." He caught himself before asking a personal question about Mandy.

Christina laughed. "Does she what?"

"Never mind." Tony slowed down, and Christina glanced

at him before meeting his stride. "Are you upset about something?" he asked.

"No," she said quickly. "But I have to admit, my sister deserves to be the manager."

"We have other plans for her future."

"Other plans?" she said with sarcasm. "They better be good ones, or I'm sure another company will snatch her right up."

"I'll keep that in mind." He certainly didn't want to lose Mandy.

"Good." She laughed. "Fortunately for you, Mandy doesn't hold grudges like I do. She says I need to move on and not let other people get me down, but I can't help it, no matter how much I pray about it." When she stopped talking, he glanced over at her in time to see her chew on her bottom lip. She blinked before looking back at him, then smiled. "You're a Christian, right?"

"Yes," he said. "I have been all my life."

"Us, too. Our parents said they couldn't always give us the things we wanted, but they fed us, made sure we had plenty of love, and took us to church every Sunday."

He wanted to ask more questions about Mandy, but this didn't seem like the right time. "Your family sounds quite a bit like mine," he said as they reached the parking lot. "I gotta run, but maybe we can resume this conversation at another time, okay?"

She nodded. "Don't tell my sister I blabbed so much. She hates when I can't keep my mouth shut."

That was a good thing to know for the future—in case he couldn't find out about Mandy on his own. He offered what he hoped was a reassuring grin. "Your secret's safe with me."

❧

The rest of the afternoon and evening were busy beyond anything Mandy had ever experienced. She had one appointment after another—a couple of them even overlapping. Fortunately, she'd juggled a busy schedule long enough to not get rattled.

After her last client left, and she was closing out the

register for the night, Brent walked in. "You sure have been slammed," he said. "I kept waiting for things to lighten up over here to talk to you."

She wished he'd waited until tomorrow, but she didn't want to be rude. "So what can I help you with, Brent?"

"Oh, nothing," he began as he glanced around the room before turning back to face her. "Okay, I might as well come clean. I met Christina today, and I'd like to get to know her better. I thought you might give me some helpful hints."

"Just be yourself, and you'll do fine."

"You sure that'll work? In case you haven't noticed, I'm not exactly the smoothest guy in town."

"There are other, more important things than being smooth," Mandy said. "If being yourself doesn't work, then it's not meant to be."

"Are you almost ready to leave?" he asked. "I'll walk you to your car."

"Sure, let me finish here and I can go."

As they walked out together, he asked some questions about her sister. Mandy explained that Christina was looking for a job.

"Yeah, she told me. We have a full staff, so I wasn't much help. However, Tony said he was hoping to add some people to Small World. Is there a nepotism policy with your company?"

"I doubt it, but I'm not so sure she'd want to work with me." They stopped when they got to her car.

"So will you put in a good word for me?" he asked.

"Even better than that, why don't you call her?" Mandy suggested. Brent was nice enough—just not someone Mandy would be interested in. Her sister, on the other hand, seemed smitten.

"If you're sure she won't mind."

Mandy dug in her purse for paper and a pen. She jotted down her parents' house line number and handed it to him. "My mom or sister will probably answer."

He took the paper, folded it, and stuck it in his pocket. "Thanks, Mandy. You sure are being understanding about things."

"What do you mean, Brent?"

"You know, after it didn't work out between you and me."

six

"Between you and me?"

He nodded. "We were just starting to get to know each other, but when Christina came into the picture, that was it for me."

Mandy had to squelch a giggle. Mandy had never been attracted to Brent, so if he liked Christina, that was a good thing—and a relief.

Well, wasn't it? Protectiveness toward her sister overtook the relief.

"Why are you looking at me like that?" he asked.

"Ya know, Brent, I don't really know that much about you. Do you go to church?"

He shuffled his feet and looked down at them before meeting her gaze. "I used to, back when I was a kid, but I have to admit, I haven't been in a while."

"My family is committed to our faith," Mandy said. "Christina might not agree, but I think one of the reasons she came back to West Virginia was to reconnect to family and get her Christian bearings again."

"Wow." Brent looked happier than she expected. "She's not only a looker, she's a nice Christian girl! I hit the jackpot with this one."

The guy was clearly missing something. "How do you figure that?"

"Look at her," he said. "Maybe it's hard for you to see this since you're her sister, but she's gorgeous. The problem with that, though, is the pretty girls aren't always the ones you want meeting your family." He paused and gave her a conspiratorial look. "Know what I mean?"

"I think so." She forced herself to suppress a groan at his assumptions.

"She's smart, too."

Mandy was surprised at that last comment. She agreed that Christina was smart, but not only did she not often show it, most people couldn't get past the pretty face.

"Just remember that my sister is still trying to find herself, but she's not going to do anything to compromise her Christian faith."

Brent held up his hands and gave her a serious expression. "Oh, I wouldn't ever ask her to do that. By the way, where does your family go to church?"

She told him the name and location. After they parted ways, she laughed. Looked like their church was about to experience some sudden exponential growth.

The next morning, Tony frowned at her as she approached the studio door. "You weren't scheduled until noon," he said.

She was so used to opening every day, she forgot to check the schedule. "Oops." Stopping in her tracks, she tried to figure out what to do now.

Tony's frown turned to a sympathetic smile. "Look, I have some stuff to do. If you'd like to swap mornings, I'm fine with it."

"You don't mind?"

"Not at all. In fact, having you here now makes my life a lot easier."

"What day do you want me to come late?"

He glanced over the schedule then looked up. "How about tomorrow? My sister and her kids are coming to town in the morning, so if you work later tomorrow, I'll be able to spend some time with them."

The fact that he was a family guy made him likable, but she tried to stifle the thought. But she had to admit, her first negative internal reaction to him was long gone by now.

"How many children does your sister have?"

"Two," he replied. "A girl and a boy—both in elementary school. Any ideas for activities they might like?"

She thought for a moment then remembered where some

of her clients took their kids. "How about the Children's Museum?"

"Where is it?"

After giving him the address, she added, "It's small, but our customers seem to enjoy it."

"Thanks, Mandy. You really are special. I can't imagine this place without you."

"Thanks, Tony."

"You're good at everything—with kids, keeping this place running, your sister—everything."

"Not everything."

"Everything that matters." Tony reached out and lightly touched her arm then pulled back as though he thought he'd made a mistake. Then he put away what he'd been working on and walked toward the door as he cleared his throat. "I'll have my cell phone on, so if you need anything, just call."

Mandy swallowed hard and nodded. She bit back the automatic response that she'd been handling everything just fine without him.

"Oh, Mandy, before I forget, I wanted to talk to you about some things that came up during the management conference call. We need to schedule a meeting—like when we're slow around here, or I can bring in a part-timer to handle the front desk. There's a lot of information that I think pertains to you."

She couldn't imagine what, since she'd been overlooked as manager. Unless. . . *Uh-oh.* "There is?"

He nodded. "Yes, and I think you'll like it." Tony pulled on his jacket. "We'll discuss all that later. If I'm going to get this stuff done and be back so you can leave early, I gotta run."

"That's okay. You don't have to—"

"One of the things we talked about was working too much. We want you to take some time off."

"Oh." Mandy lowered her head.

"See ya."

After he left, she rested her elbows on the counter and buried her face in her hands. Tony's take-charge personality left her feeling out of sorts.

The phone rang several times, one of the calls being her mother. "Have you thought about a place where Christina can work?"

"Mom, I know this is important to you and Dad, but give her some time, okay?"

"She listens to you," her mother said.

Mandy disagreed, but this wasn't the time or place to argue. "I'll keep my eyes open, but if you really want to help her, maybe you can advise her to call a temp agency to line her up with a temp-to-perm job."

After she hung up, Mandy finished organizing the files. She only had one photo session before Tony returned. He brought lunch.

"I thought that since we were slow, we could talk today. We can use the front office, and I'll leave the door open so we can see if anyone comes in."

Right when they sat down, a woman walked in with a pair of toddlers. Mandy jumped up and headed straight for the desk, with Tony right behind her. Tony offered to work the camera, but Mandy insisted she could handle it.

"What if I promise to keep my hands off the props?" he whispered.

"And candy?" she countered with a playful grin.

"That, too."

"Well. . ." She glanced around, pretending to ponder, then directed her gaze at him. The second their eyes met, her insides lurched, and she wished she hadn't looked at Tony. "Um, sure, that's fine."

An hour later, when she was finished, she went to the front desk and pulled up the company order forms on the computer. A message popped up, alerting her that the page no longer existed. She marched straight to Tony's office.

Tony was on the phone. "Sure, I'll do that. . .yes, that's

right." He glanced up and pointed to the chair across from him. When she didn't sit, he frowned but glanced away. He wrapped up his conversation in less than a minute then looked back at Mandy. "What's up?"

"I just tried to order some supplies, but the company order form is no longer there."

"That's one of the things I wanted to discuss," he said. "They weren't supposed to change that until next week, though. What all did you need to order? I'll take care of it."

She handed him her list. "Is *everything* changing around here?"

"Pretty much, yes."

Mandy's shoulders fell as her breath escaped her lungs. "Looks like I'll need to be totally retrained."

"Everyone will." As Tony looked down at the paper in front of him, she noticed the anxiety on his face. "The company is in the process of restructuring."

❧

Tony felt awful that he couldn't share more with Mandy yet. Uncle Ed had made him privy to some company changes, but he wasn't at liberty to discuss any of them—not even the ones that involved Mandy's future with the company. They hadn't finished hammering out the details yet, which complicated everything for him at the store level. But he couldn't be too secretive with Mandy—not after all she'd done for the company. He'd have another talk with Uncle Ed and Ricco.

"I—uh, I guess I'll go back out to the front and get ready for my next photo session," she said as she shuffled backward, out of the office.

The second she was gone, he picked up the phone and punched in the number of the regional manager. His cousin Ricco answered on the first ring.

"I need to talk to Mandy soon," Tony said. "She knows there are changes, and I can tell she's worried."

"Look, Tony," Ricco said in his understanding but firm

voice. "I know this is tough on you, but we don't have anything firm to tell her yet. Have you discussed the changes in the first rollout?"

"Not yet. We haven't had the opportunity to sit down and discuss it."

"As long as you're both doing your jobs, I don't see what the problem is. Go ahead and tell her about the first phase."

Ricco had been away from the trenches so long, he obviously didn't remember all the interruptions. Ricco had never wanted to work for Small World, but when Tony left for the army, Ricco's dad, who promised it would be temporary, pressured him into it. Last they had talked, right after Tony got out of the army, Ricco said he actually liked the job now—especially since they were making some of the changes he'd wanted since he started.

"Okay, I'll just have to get one of the part-timers to come in early."

"You have the budget to hire another full-timer," Ricco reminded him. "There are plenty of people out there looking for jobs. Why don't you hire one of them?"

Tony wanted Mandy's input during the hiring process, but he couldn't very well do that before telling her about the changes. "It takes time to find the right fit, Ricco."

"You're right. It does." He chuckled. "You really like Mandy, don't you?"

"Of course I do. And I'd like to discuss Mandy's options." Tony knew his persistence could get on Ricco's nerves, but he was willing to take his chances. "She's worked so hard to keep this place running smoothly, and I'm sure she's frustrated."

"Are you saying she's got an attitude?" Ricco asked. "Because if that's the case, maybe we should rethink—"

"No, that's not what I'm saying. Mandy has been professional at all times. I just don't want to risk losing her."

"It won't be too much longer. Just tell her what you can now, and let her know we haven't forgotten about her." Ricco paused before adding, "If you want her input, let her know that, too. Maybe it'll appease her until you have something more concrete to share."

Tony doubted that. Mandy was a smart woman who'd see through any actions designed to hide the fact that she wouldn't get what she wanted.

When it was almost time for Mandy to go home, Tony took advantage of the few minutes of quiet. "I'll get Bella or Steve to come in, so you and I can have a meeting."

"Will this be a regular thing now?" she asked. "Even when Parker was still the manager, we never had meetings."

Tony racked his brain as he tried to think of a way to explain without saying more than he should. "I'm not big on meetings, either, but I do need to let you know some new corporate policies and decisions."

"Can't you just tell me now?"

"No, it's sort of complicated, and you'll probably have some questions." He paused before adding, "I don't want to get started and then be interrupted again."

She pursed her lips, tightened her jaw, and offered a clipped nod. "Okay." The resignation in her voice let him know she didn't completely trust him, but she knew who was in charge. That hurt.

After she was gone, Tony rubbed the back of his neck. Now all he cared about was making Mandy understand and gaining her trust.

❧

For the first time since working at Small World, Mandy couldn't get out of there fast enough. Her job was about to change, but the only change she'd wanted was the promotion.

Mandy needed to talk to someone, but not her sister or parents. Her best friend, Dahlia, had moved to Chicago, so she decided to call her.

"Maybe you expect too much," Dahlia said. "You've always worked so hard but never tooted your own horn. If you don't let people know what you want, don't expect them to read your mind."

After they got off the phone, Mandy thought about expectations. Were hers unrealistic? She hadn't even dated since college because no one measured up to what she thought she wanted.

She had a tough time falling asleep, but when she finally did, she dreamed about Tony. The next morning, she got ready for work knowing he wouldn't be there because his sister was in town.

There were so many walk-ins that morning, the hours went by in a blur. She'd barely finished with her last family before lunch, when she glanced up and spotted Tony walking toward the studio. He sure looked handsome in his charcoal gray pinstriped suit. Flanked by a woman holding the hand of a little boy on one side and a little girl on the other, he would have made an excellent model for a dad on his way to have his family's pictures taken.

"Hey, Mandy, I'd like for you to meet my sister, Angela."

The attractive woman with the shoulder-length dark hair extended her hand. "I'm so happy to meet you, Mandy. Tony has said many nice things about you."

Tony nudged her. "Shh. Don't tell her my secrets."

"What secrets?" Angela said playfully before turning back to Mandy. "He said you were the best thing that ever happened to Small World Portrait Studio and that if you weren't here, his job would be miserable." She wiggled her eyebrows. "He also told me you were very family oriented— just like us." After smiling at Mandy, she turned to Tony. "And you're right. She's beautiful."

Tony lifted both hands and let them fall to his sides, clearly pretending to be annoyed. "Well, there ya go. Anything you want to know, just ask my sister."

"Thank you." Mandy laughed, in spite of the heat that had crept up her face. "It's nice to meet you, too, Angela. Are you here to have your children's pictures taken?"

Angela grinned and winked at her brother. "And she's an excellent salesperson, too." She turned back to Mandy. "Not today. I just wanted to meet you after all the nice things Tony said. He told me about the Children's Museum, so I thought we'd go there."

After Angela left, Tony went back to his office before coming out with a stack of papers. "Going somewhere important?" she asked.

seven

Tony nodded. "Chamber of commerce meeting. It won't be a long one, though," he said. "I'll be back this afternoon."

He walked toward the door, turned around to face her, and paused. She had the feeling he wanted to say something, but he didn't. He just lifted a hand and waved before walking away.

Mandy barely had time to gather her thoughts before the next family arrived. She got the children in place, snapped their pictures, and arranged the computer proofs without any trouble.

"Mommy, look what the nice lady gave me!" the youngest of the three boys said.

The woman looked at the plastic dinosaur Mandy had pulled from her bag, then glanced up, grinned, and mouthed, "Thanks."

Mandy smiled then refocused her attention on the computer proofs. The children had been extremely good for her once she got their attention, but they were bundles of energy. She had a tremendous amount of respect for mothers—particularly those with more than one small child.

She worked as quickly as possible before the children's attention spans ran out. Finally, she motioned for the mom to come take a look.

"I wanna see!" the middle boy said.

Mandy pulled a couple of step stools out from behind the counter. "How's this?"

The two older boys each took a stool, and the mother picked up the smallest child. Mandy handed the mother the mouse and encouraged her to let the boys help.

It didn't take long for them to agree on a package. "Thank

you so much," the mother said. "My husband will appreciate the fact that I didn't spend a fortune, since we just had pictures taken six months ago."

She spotted Tony walking toward the door. It took all her concentration to keep her mind off his presence as he came in.

"We want you to come back." Mandy pulled out a coupon for the family's next visit. "Put this someplace safe and use it toward your next photo session."

"You're amazing with people," Tony observed. "I'd like to take you to the next chamber of commerce meeting with me."

Her sister called, so Tony went back to his office to give her some space. "Hi, what's up?"

"Mom and Dad are really after me to get a job."

"I agree with them," Mandy said.

"It's not that easy. I've e-mailed and sent my résumé to a few places."

"You have to put a lot of effort into a job hunt."

"If those people in Hollywood weren't so mean, I'd have an acting job."

"But you're not in Hollywood anymore. You're in Wheeling, West Virginia, where hardworking, decent people live."

"I can work hard," Christina said. "Someone just has to give me a chance."

"I'm getting off early tonight. Why don't you come to my apartment after dinner?"

"Mom said she'd fix dinner, and I can bring you some."

"When did she say that?"

"When she told me to call you and see if I could come over one night this week. Sorry."

Mandy chuckled. So she'd been set up, and she'd fallen right into the trap. But that was okay. This was for a good cause.

"Perfect. I'll call you when I leave here."

A half hour later, Tony came walking into the studio. "I just heard from Ricco. He's scheduling a meeting for you." He breezed past her on his way to the back before he stopped and added, "In Atlanta."

"When?"

"As soon as possible." Weird. He wouldn't look her in the eye.

"Do you know what it's all about?"

"I'm not at liberty to say." He edged away from her. "But I do know they want you there in two weeks."

"Two weeks?"

"Yeah, and he wants you to go over to the store in Pittsburgh to show the new photographer some tips on getting the children to cooperate."

"When?"

"This afternoon."

Before she had a chance to say another word, he'd left her alone with the cameras.

She rounded the corner, where she spotted him punching some numbers into the phone. He was clearly avoiding conversation with her, so she backed away.

Rather than press Tony for answers, she decided to wait until she met with Ricco in two weeks. She gathered her things, stopped at the desk, and stared at him until he looked up at her. She needed to brief him on the children he'd be photographing. "The little girl is diabetic, so their mother doesn't want either of them having sugar. She'll smile for the purple dinosaur, and her brother likes action figures."

"I can handle them," Tony said. He managed a slight smile and a glance in her direction. "Especially now that I know I won't have to handle the candy." He leaned back in his chair, still looking at her. "Seriously, Mandy, I appreciate your concern for this place, but I promise I won't mess things up too bad."

She pursed her lips and nodded. He was right. She did need to let go.

"You don't have to come back this afternoon," he added.

Mandy opened her mouth but decided it was pointless to say anything. On the way to the studio in Pittsburgh, all sorts of things flitted through Mandy's mind. Why the urgency of helping this new photographer? She'd heard he'd had his own studio for years.

Right when she pulled into a parking spot, her cell phone rang. It was Tony.

"Are you there yet?" he asked.

"I just got here, but I'm still in the parking lot."

"I wanted to warn you that Ricco is there. The new photographer has never worked with children before, and he threatened to quit. We needed someone, and he's got a tremendous amount of experience, as well as a name in the area, and Ricco wanted to give him a chance. I told Ricco to give you some time with him, and he agreed."

"I don't get why he needed a job if he was so good or why he was hired if he had no experience with kids."

"People couldn't afford his prices, and he waited too long to drop them, so his business folded. Don't bring this up to anyone, but I think he begged, and they were desperate for a photographer. At least his background checked out, so I think he's trainable."

A nervous chuckle escaped her lips. "That's good."

"I didn't want you to be surprised. As for the meeting at the home office—well, try to relax and let things happen as they're supposed to. Ricco's a good guy. He knows what a valuable employee you are."

"I'll try."

"I asked him to explain some stuff while you're in Pittsburgh, and he said he would."

"I appreciate that."

"I said a prayer for you."

"Thank you, Tony."

Mandy squeezed her eyes shut and prayed that she could remain calm, no matter what Ricco wanted to discuss. She opened her eyes and took several deep breaths. She wished she'd worn something a little nicer, but at least there was nothing offensive about black slacks and a white-collared blouse. Boring, as Christina would say, but not offensive.

She shoved the door open and walked into the reception area where she was greeted by Peggy, who'd helped her when she first started with the company. Peggy lifted a hand and waved. "Come on back, and I'll introduce you to James, the new photographer." She lowered her voice and added, "He's a little out of sorts today, so don't be too upset by anything he says. Want some coffee?"

"No thanks." Mandy smiled at Peggy then looked around at the photos covering the walls.

The hallway was wide but short, so they didn't have to go far. The studio was bigger than the one in Wheeling, but everything else was basically the same.

"Children these days are so bad! How can you expect me to get decent portraits of them?" He flailed his arms. "They need to listen."

Ricco sat on a stool across from the ranting man. He glanced up and waved as he spotted her.

"C'mon back, Mandy," he said as he gestured.

She gulped hard and did as he asked. She felt her cheeks flush.

"Mandy, this is James, one of the best photographers in Pennsylvania. He recently decided to shut down his studio, so we talked him into working for us."

Mandy extended her hand as she realized how Ricco was trying to flatter James while he was there. "Nice to meet you, James."

He reluctantly shook hands with her. "So you're the one everyone's raving about."

"I am?"

Ricco let out a nervous laugh. "Yes, you've developed quite a reputation for getting kids to cooperate."

"It's just a matter of getting down on their level and figuring out what they like."

Ricco got off his stool and took a couple of steps toward the front. "I'll leave the two of you to talk. Come see me when you're done, Mandy."

After Mandy got an earful of how terrible he thought the working conditions were, she gave James a few helpful hints.

When his appointment arrived, she even showed him how to position the children and get them to smile. He resisted at first, but after a couple of awkward attempts, he succeeded in getting them to behave. Once he had the children under control, the session was great.

After the children went to the front to wait, James shook his head. "No wonder they like you so much, Mandy. Thanks. Maybe I'll give this a little more time before I make my decision about staying or leaving." He pointed toward the office area. "Ricco wants to talk to you now."

Mandy found her way back to the office where Ricco waited for her. "Have a seat." He glanced down at some paperwork on the desk, until she got settled. "Tony gave you a glowing report. Says you were doing a great job of running the studio single-handedly before he arrived."

Mandy smiled. "I did the best I could."

"We appreciate all your hard work. Unfortunately, while we've been in the process of reorganizing, we overlooked some important details."

"I understand." Her voice came out much weaker than she wanted, so she cleared her throat.

"The company is still in a state of change, but we have some thoughts about how to utilize your skills."

Mandy blinked. This sounded like a good thing. She leaned forward, hoping to hear that she was under consideration for a promotion—or at least something concrete.

"But unfortunately, we haven't ironed everything out yet." He offered an apologetic smile as he tapped the end of his pencil on the desk. "There are two reasons I wanted to bring you in. First, we needed you to spend some time with James. How did that go?"

"Okay, I think. His photography skills are obviously there, but I think his pride was getting in his way."

Ricco's eyebrows lifted as he nodded. "Good observation."

"Only time will tell, but he just needed some kid tips."

Ricco laughed. "Your specialty. This can't be easy for him

after having his own studio for so long." He steepled his fingers. "Next, I'd like for you to clear your schedule for the week after next, so you can spend some time at the home office in Atlanta." He typed something into the computer then glanced back at her. "Will that be a problem?"

She shook her head. "No, that's fine. I can go then."

"The other reason is that I'd like for you to help Tony interview prospective photographers to help you in the studio. Have you ever been involved in the hiring process before?"

Again, Mandy shook her head. "No, Bella and Steve had already been hired when I started."

"They've both asked Tony if they can cut their hours, so we really need to find some people to replace them. Tony can fill you in, until we have a chance to work on the interview manual." He typed some more then glanced up at Mandy. "How does that sound?"

"They never told me they wanted to cut their hours."

"They probably didn't want to leave you in a lurch. So how about it?"

She smiled. "It sounds fine."

"I wanted to make sure you had some of the basics before you screen potential applicants. Give me a minute to print some of the information, so we can go over it. I was going to do this before you got here, but with James threatening to leave, that had to come first."

She forced a smile. "I can imagine." After a short pause, she added, "Do you really think he would have left?"

"No." Ricco gave her conspiratorial look. "But we don't want him to be miserable, so I thought seeing you in action might inspire him. I went over some of my ideas with Tony, and he thought you'd have the insight to know what we're looking for in photographers."

"I think I have a pretty good idea."

"Mainly, they need to know how to deal with kids." He smiled. "Obviously."

Mandy grinned back. "True."

After the printer spit out several pages, he looked them over, stapled them, and handed them across the desk. "We have to follow some hiring policies," he explained. "I want to make sure you understand what we're allowed or not allowed to say, according to the law."

Mandy sat there and followed along as he went over the legal issues. Some of it she knew, and other stuff made sense. When he got to the last paragraph, he looked up at her.

"Any questions?" he asked.

She shook her head. "No, not really."

"Are you comfortable interviewing prospective photographers?"

She pondered that question for a moment before nodding. Interviewing people who would be hired in at the same level as her made no sense, but she'd do it if that was what they wanted. Finally, she squared her shoulders, looked him in the eye, and nodded. "I'm fine with that."

"Good." Ricco stood and smiled. "I'm glad you're on our team, Mandy. We're very impressed with your work. Tony is especially impressed."

"Thank you." She shook hands with him and got out of there as quickly as she could. Tony had said not to come back into the office, which was a relief. The emotional weight of the meeting had worn her out.

Mandy kicked off her shoes as soon as she got home. She picked up the TV remote and did some channel surfing, but there wasn't anything on TV that interested her. Finally, she gave up and picked out a CD to listen to. The ringing phone jolted her.

"I tried calling you at work, but Tony said you weren't coming back in," Christina said.

"He told me I didn't need to after I left the regional office."

"Mind if I come over now? I really need to talk."

Mandy sighed. Even though she'd agreed for Christina to come, she really didn't feel like having company, but she couldn't very well turn down her sister. "Sure, that's fine."

"You don't have to sound so mad."

"I'm not mad," Mandy replied. "Just tired."

"Good thing you won't have to cook. Mom loaded up some food, and she's letting me use her car. I've got some great news. See ya in a few minutes." She hung up before Mandy had a chance to say another word.

Mandy went through her apartment and straightened up a few things, put her work shoes in the closet, and shoved her feet into some clogs. By the time Christina knocked at her door, she was mentally ready for her sister.

"You're not gonna believe this, Mandy!"

"I'm sure I won't. What happened?"

"I got an e-mail back on a job I applied for online, and you'll never guess where I'm interviewing in a couple of days."

"Where?" Mandy tried to sound enthusiastic, but she was still too drained.

"I answered a blind ad for a management training job, and it's with Small World Portrait Studio!"

eight

"A management training job at Small World?" Mandy's throat tightened.

Christina couldn't contain her excitement. "I answered a bunch of ads at online job sites, and I heard back from Small World. Isn't that the coolest?"

Mandy chewed her lip for a moment before slowly shaking her head. "I don't think that's such a good idea—you and me working together." Her body had gone numb.

"Oh, it's not a problem," Christina said. "I called the number they sent me and talked to someone who said it's okay with them to have more than one family member working there."

That wasn't the point, but Mandy didn't want to upset her sister, and she certainly wasn't about to dampen her enthusiasm for getting a job. "So who did you talk to?"

"Some lady named Peggy. She said she knows you."

Mandy nodded as she wondered why Peggy never mentioned talking to Christina. "She works in the Pittsburgh office."

"She's very nice, in spite of the fact that I called her when she was about to leave."

That explained it. Peggy talked to Christina after she left.

"What else did she say?"

Christina sat down and clasped her hands together as she looked up at the ceiling. "She put me on the phone with some guy named Ricco who told me they were looking for trainees—that they're putting together a management training program for people who are willing to relocate."

"Do you have an interview lined up yet?"

Christina made a face. "I have to take an aptitude test, then they'll interview me. They want me to talk to a bunch of people."

"When and where are you supposed to take the test?"

"First thing tomorrow in Pittsburgh!" Christina leaned forward. "They'll have the results within a few minutes after I finish, and if I pass, I'll get to interview at your studio!"

Mandy felt a groan coming on, but she stifled it. "Have you told Mom and Dad?"

"Of course, and they're thrilled, although Dad warned me that I need to act all professional, or I might mess things up for you." She tilted her head and pouted. "I can't believe he would say something so mean. I'd never do anything to hurt you, Mandy."

Guilt set in as Mandy realized she'd thought the same thing. She smiled and tried to dig deep for a positive angle as she reached for her sister's hands. "I know you wouldn't." *At least not intentionally.* "Just make sure you're honest on the test and give direct answers during the interview."

"Hey, I have an idea! Why don't we do a practice interview?"

Mandy's stomach rumbled. "Let's eat first."

She got plates and sat down at the table. Christina folded her hands. "I'll say the blessing."

Mandy bowed her head as her sister thanked God for the food and the possibility of being able to work together. When she opened her eyes, she felt a wave of remorse wash over her. At that moment, she realized how her control issues had affected her.

Christina tilted her head. "Are you okay?"

With her lips between her teeth, Mandy slowly nodded. She sucked in a deep breath and looked down as she let it out. "I want to apologize for being so bossy."

"Bossy?" Christina laughed. "Isn't that what big sisters are supposed to be?"

"Forgive me, okay?"

"Of course. So what kinds of questions are on this test?" Christina asked.

"I have no idea," Mandy replied. "When I was hired, after the background check, all I had to do was get through the probationary period without messing anything up. But then I wasn't hired to be in management."

A look of shock popped onto Christina's face. "Don't tell me I'm training to be your boss."

Mandy felt sick to her stomach. "I don't know what you'll be training for—that is, if you get hired."

"I'm so sorry. If you don't want me to do this, just say so. I was so excited about being able to work with you, this never dawned on me."

"That's okay," Mandy said. "If I have another new boss, it might as well be you. At least I know you love me no matter what."

Christina offered a sympathetic smile. "I've got your back, Mandy. You've always been there for me, and I'd love to do whatever I can for you."

After they ate, Mandy grabbed the plates and set them in the sink. "Since you have to get up early, I'll take care of cleaning up."

"I don't mind helping." Christina had already picked up her handbag and taken a step toward the door.

"Thanks, but I'll be fine. Get some sleep and don't worry about the interview."

Christina's eyes widened. "We didn't practice interviewing."

"I don't think you need to practice. Just answer the questions honestly and be direct. I'm sure everyone will love you."

After her sister left, Mandy sat down with her Bible and flipped through to some passages that had always gotten her through difficult times in the past. She settled on Psalm 25. She'd always thought of herself as a committed Christian, but it was time she accepted that her true thoughts and actions didn't reflect it. She needed to work on trust in His Word.

❧

Tony got to work early the next morning. When Ricco told him about Mandy's sister interviewing, he wondered how

Mandy would feel, and it kept him up all night.

The sound of the door signaled Mandy's arrival. He stood, took a deep breath, sent up a plea for divine guidance, then walked out to greet Mandy. One look at her face let him know something was different.

He smiled. "Hi there. How was your meeting with Ricco?"

She bobbed her head. "It was good. He basically just went over interviewing techniques for new photographers."

"In the future, you'll be screening them before I talk to them."

"That's what he said."

"Mandy, I heard that your sister applied for a job here, and she's coming later, after her interview with Ricco."

"Why didn't you say something?"

"I didn't find out until last night, when Ricco called. He sounded excited about it."

"Good."

"Wanna talk about it?"

Her expression concerned him. "Not really."

This was going to be a very long day. "I saw that you have several appointments this morning, but you have some free time this afternoon."

She remained at the door and just stood there staring at him. She wasn't smiling, but her lips naturally turned up at the corners. Tony had no doubt she wasn't aware of how gorgeous she was.

"What time is Christina coming in?" she asked.

"Right after lunch. I thought you and I could interview her together since it'll be your first time, sort of a practice session for you."

"She told me this is for a management training position."

Tony nodded. "That's part of the company restructuring. They want full-timers to be well rounded, so they're bringing them in with more of an opportunity for advancement."

He wasn't sure what he should do. If she was upset, he wanted to comfort her, but this wasn't the time or place, and he couldn't overstep the bounds of company policy—even those he disagreed with. The changes had clearly thrown her off-kilter.

"So how many managers will we have in this office?" she asked, still not smiling.

"Just one. The person who will officially be in management training will learn photography, how to manage the books, and other company policies. After that, we're not sure. The ad says the person has to be willing to relocate."

Mandy chewed her bottom lip for a moment before she slowly nodded. "So I suppose you'll need me to help with the photography training."

"Yes."

"Okay, then." She swung around and walked away, leaving him standing there feeling like a heel.

❧

Mandy was confused by everything—all the changes that seemed to have taken place overnight. She hadn't seen any of this coming, which was her own fault. If she'd had more contact with the home office before Tony arrived, things might have been different. Instead, she'd kept her nose to her tasks, making sure the studio ran smoothly—and she'd done an excellent job, according to what both Tony and Ricco had said.

She remembered her prayers from the night before. It was time to put all her trust in God and stop trying to take it all on herself.

She stayed busy all morning. Tony popped into the darkened studio and let her know he'd gotten lunch for both of them. "I'll be in my office," he said. "Come on back when you're done."

After she finished showing proofs to her last client of the morning, she joined Tony. "You didn't have to do this," she said. "I could have run out to the deli and picked up something quick."

"What's going on with you?" he asked, his voice barely above a whisper. "Are you upset about something?"

She shrugged as she tried not to show her anger. "Not really."

"You are. I can tell." He stared at her until she met his gaze. "Are you unhappy about your sister coming in for an interview?"

Mandy's body tensed. She wasn't ready to talk about her feelings just yet. "Not unhappy, but things aren't always as they seem."

"I know, Mandy. Please trust me. Some things are out of my control." He reached for her hand but quickly dropped his hand to his side.

There was that *trust* word. She saw the tightness in his face, letting her know he felt awful about what was happening—or not happening. Mandy shrugged. "I understand. I'll be okay." She needed more time to think about things before she said or did anything she might later regret.

He chuckled nervously as he gestured toward the food. "I got chicken, turkey, and tuna. Take your pick."

"Turkey would be good."

He handed her a wrapped sandwich. "I realize there are probably some family dynamics going on. I want you to know that we won't evaluate you based on your sister's performance, and the same goes for her."

Mandy slowly unwrapped her sandwich as she thought about what he'd said. "If my sister winds up being the manager here, will she be my supervisor?" She tried to keep the question matter-of-fact, but she wasn't sure she succeeded.

"No," he said. "In fact, the only working relationship you'll have is that you'll be training her in photography. Once she's ready to move up, we'll know more about where you'll be."

She almost choked on her first bite. "Are you saying I might be moved?"

His face tightened. "Don't look too far ahead, Mandy. Once we get to that point, we'll deal with it."

The phone rang, so Tony answered it. She only heard his side of the conversation, but she could tell it was about

Christina. After he hung up, he lifted his eyebrows and folded his hands.

"Your sister is a very smart woman. She scored very well on the aptitude test."

"That's good."

"It is. Small World hired a company to help us screen potential employees based on a balance of basic aptitude and ability to think on their feet. And that's what I wanted to discuss with you. Have you had a chance to go over the interview questions?"

"Ricco and I went over them yesterday."

"Good," Tony said. "What we need to do is plan a strategy for the interview before Christina arrives. Since she's your sister, I'm sure it'll be a little different for you." He leaned forward and held her gaze. "But the outcome has nothing to do with your employment here."

Mandy didn't have anything to say, so she nodded. She listened to Tony as he explained how they were going to tag team the interview.

"You start with the basics then turn her over to me. I'll let you sit in on the entire interview, so you'll know what to do next time."

The buzzer on the door sounded, and they both turned toward the front. It was Mandy's next appointment.

"When you come out of the session, I'll take over and show the proofs while you talk to your sister."

❧

Tony watched Mandy leave his office, her shoulders drooping a tad. He wished he'd stood up to Ricco and requested Christina's interview at another studio. But it was too late now. Mandy's feelings mattered more to him than anything at the moment.

Christina arrived as Mandy came out of the studio with the children. He nodded for the sisters to use his office, while he stepped behind the counter to work on the proofs.

After his part of the work was done and the parents had chosen the pictures they wanted, he knocked on the door then opened it. Christina tossed her long blond hair over her shoulder and grinned at him.

"This is so cool!" she said. "Who'd have thought I'd get to interview with my own sister for a job?"

"Yes, it's very cool," he said as he worked hard to keep from smiling.

Mandy looked comfortable behind the desk, her hands folded in front of her, the list of questions beside them. "I've gone over the company's expectations and discussed the first five questions."

He looked at Christina. "So what do you think so far? Is this something you think you'd like to pursue?"

She nodded with enthusiasm. "My sister loves her job, so I'm sure I'd like it, too!"

Tony glanced over at Mandy, who now looked amused. A surge of relief flooded him. "Excellent! Now let's get on with the rest of the interview."

After Christina left the office, Mandy hopped up out of the manager's chair. "I should have let you sit there," she said, "but I wasn't thinking clearly."

"You were fine." They held a gaze for several seconds. "Perfect, in fact." So perfect his heart pounded nearly out of control. If he didn't keep his feelings in check, he knew he could fall hard for Mandy.

"Now what?"

"We turn our interview notes over to Ricco and let him make the decision. Of course, we have to make separate evaluations, and we're not supposed to discuss it until after we fill out our separate forms."

"This is almost scientific, isn't it?" she asked.

"As much as an interview can be." He handed her another form. "Since no one is scheduled to come in, why don't we do this now?"

She took the paper and left him alone in the office. Fifteen minutes later, she returned and placed the sealed envelope with the form on his desk. "All done."

The phone rang, so Mandy left to answer it at the front desk. It was Christina.

"Well? How'd I do? Did I get the job?"

"You just left here."

"How long does it take to decide whether or not you want to hire me?"

"It's not that easy," Mandy explained. "Tony and I had to fill out forms from your interview, then someone from the home office will look them over. You'll have to come back for another interview."

"That's silly," Christina said. "It's just a job."

"It won't be long," Mandy assured her. "Just remember that the interview works both ways. They're interviewing you to see if they think you'll be a good fit for the company, and you're interviewing them to see if it's a place you'd like to work."

"I already told you, if you work there, it must be good."

"If it's meant to be, it'll work out." After Mandy got off the phone, she leaned against the counter and closed her eyes to ask the Lord for clarity.

"Are you okay?"

nine

Tony's voice startled her. Mandy opened her eyes in time to see him standing about a foot away. She felt a catch in her throat.

He took a step back. "Oh, sorry. I thought you might not be feeling well. I didn't realize you were praying."

"That's okay." Now that he wasn't so close, she could look at him without the flutter. "My sister just called and wanted to know how long it'll be before she has an answer."

"I wish I knew." He shoved his hands into his pockets and grinned down at her. "They're being ultracautious. Apparently, they made some hiring mistakes in other studios, and they want to make sure they do everything they can to avoid that in the future."

"Oh, I understand." Mandy paused before deciding to come right out with the question that had been gnawing at her since Tony had arrived. She was trusting the Lord, but she still wanted an answer. "Is there any reason why I'm not being considered for this management training position?"

❧

Tony had been waiting for this. He had no doubt Mandy would make an excellent studio manager, but the position they'd made for her was even better.

"You know I can't discuss it."

"Is it because they don't think I can do it?"

"I didn't say that. You asked if there was a reason you weren't being considered for *this* management training position, and I answered you." He narrowed his eyes and tried to communicate without coming out and telling her anything.

She studied his face then pulled her bottom lip between her teeth. He'd seen her do this when she was deep in thought.

"There just might be something else," he said softly. "Something better."

Mandy gave him a quizzical look. "I can't imagine what that would be, but okay, I get it. You won't betray the confidence, and that's being a good company man."

Her comment hit him wrong. "Mandy, it's not that I'm just a good company man. I've already told you there are some things in the works that aren't clear yet. I don't even know the details."

"And I'll find out in Atlanta, right?"

He nodded. "That's one thing I *can* say. You'll learn everything—or most of it—during the Atlanta trip, including things I don't even know yet."

"Okay then."

With that, she turned and walked away, leaving him standing there staring at the wall as she disappeared around it.

He walked back into his office, closed the door, and picked up the phone to call Ricco. "I want to tell Mandy something," he said as soon as Ricco came on the line.

"C'mon, Tony, you have to understand why we don't want to do this yet," Ricco reminded him. "Not all of the details have been worked through, and we want to offer her a full package—not something we're not sure we can deliver."

"At least let me tell her that. I want to give her something to look forward to."

Ricco hesitated then snorted. "Oh, all right. Just make sure she knows we don't have it all worked out. I don't want her expecting something we can't deliver."

Tony thanked him and hung up. He leaned back in his chair and stared at the closed door. Ricco had a point. Once he told Mandy, she would have expectations. Tony didn't want to get her worked up, only to feel let down if things didn't turn out as he expected. He still felt like he should give her something to look forward to, so he jotted down some thoughts before getting up to see if she was available.

The door to the studio was propped open, and there were

a couple of adults in the waiting area. He made small talk with them until their children ran out with Mandy right behind them. Not everyone would have the parents' complete confidence like Mandy did. She went behind the desk to organize the computer proofs.

He walked up behind her and whispered, "As soon as you're done, I have some news."

She leaned away, tilted her head back, and looked him in the eye. "News?"

"Yes, about your trip to Atlanta. I just talked to Ricco, and—"

"How much longer?" the children's mother asked. "We're overdue for nap time."

"Just a few more minutes," she replied.

Tony stepped toward his office. "I'll leave you alone while you finish up here."

❧

Mandy thought the parents would never make up their minds. They started out wanting the economy package, but after they saw how many good shots there were, they moved up a couple of levels.

"Their grandparents will love these," the woman said. The toddler on her hip started kicking his feet and squealing, so she put him back in his stroller. "How much do I owe you?"

Mandy swiftly took the deposit, thanked the parents, and said good-bye to the children. Then she squared her shoulders and marched toward Tony's office. Funny how, until he arrived, she'd mentally made that her office.

She rapped on the door. "You had some news?"

He glanced up from his desk and pointed to the chair across the room. "Yes, have a seat."

The way he looked at her made her squirm. "Did I do something wrong?"

Tony steepled his fingers for a few seconds then smiled. "I spoke to Ricco and told him that you needed to know something. We can't continue keeping you in the dark—at least not where your future is concerned."

Mandy's stomach instantly let out a deep growl. She wrapped her arms around her midsection. "Sorry. I'm just nervous."

"Don't be." He leaned forward with his elbows propped on his desk. "The reason you weren't considered for the promotion to studio manager was that the company has something even better in mind for you."

Mandy sat up straighter. "You've already said that, but what?"

"You already know we're restructuring. They've always hired people with no photography experience if their background checks came up clean and we thought they'd be good, but they've had some consistency issues, which is why they're planning two separate tracks."

"I'm not following you."

Tony lifted an index finger. "One track will be to manage the studios." Then he lifted another finger. "The other is for photographers."

Mandy thought about it for a few seconds. "In the past, the managers were able to do photography."

"That won't change," Tony said. "However, they still need to go through training, and that's where you come in. We need someone who can teach others a system. Your methods obviously work."

"I'm still missing something."

Tony snickered as he leaned back in his chair. "They're looking at you to be a regional trainer."

Mandy opened her mouth, but she couldn't think of anything to say. The concept of regional trainer had never dawned on her.

"It will be a management position because the photographers will rely on your expertise and experience to get the quality we need."

"Interesting." It sounded good.

"Yes," Tony agreed. "I thought so, too. That's as much as they've nailed down. The details are still on the drawing board, though."

Mandy pondered the new information. "Will I be able to continue working with the kids?"

Tony shrugged. "I don't know yet. Like I said, it's all part of the restructuring, and the home office folks don't have everything figured out yet."

"So are you part of the restructuring?" she asked. "In the past, they promoted from within."

"That's another thing I'm not sure about."

Mandy lifted an eyebrow. "What do you mean?"

"As you know, I really didn't want to be a studio manager. I wanted the job I was offered before I decided to go into the army. They put my cousin Ricco in that position, and now I see that he's done better than I would have. Now they're trying to figure out what to do with me, since I've settled down and I'm ready to have a career with the family business."

"So what does all this mean?" Mandy asked.

He leaned forward again. "It means that we're in for some exciting times, and you're part of it."

The sound of someone entering the studio caught their attention. Mandy hopped up and left the office.

She took care of the walk-in customers then got the studio ready for the next scheduled appointment. Her head still spun from Tony's surprise. But before she got too dizzy, she sent up a prayer for the ability to accept the surprises as they came.

❧

Tony hadn't expected to develop feelings for Mandy. He didn't want complications, but he knew how hard it was to find the right woman—a sweet, intelligent, Christian woman—who was strong enough to handle a roomful of children. The fact that she was beautiful was a bonus.

All the way to church on Sunday—Mandy's church—he thought about what he should do. Small World didn't have antinepotism policies, but they frowned on people dating their direct employees. And since he was the nephew of one of the company founders, he had to be above reproach.

He arrived about a minute before church began, so he quickly found a chair near the door. As the first worship songs played, he had a chance to glance around the sanctuary and get a feel for the church's personality.

It appeared to be mostly twenty- and thirty-somethings, with a few forty-somethings in the mix. People were dressed business casual, and they appeared focused on what they were there for. He sighed. It felt wonderfully similar to his church in Georgia. The sanctuary was big, and most of the chairs were filled, which made it difficult to see everyone who'd come to worship. He was pretty sure Mandy was there, but he couldn't find her.

After the music, everyone sat and opened their Bibles, and the pastor read from the Old Testament, then the New Testament. They bowed their heads for the prayer before the sermon began. Pastor Chuck Waring, a gifted speaker, paced back and forth on the stage. The sermon was powerful— filled with examples of God's grace. Tony knew he'd be back; this church felt right.

He filed out of the sanctuary, shook the pastor's hand, introduced himself, and said Mandy had told him about it. "It's nice to have you here, Tony. I hope you decide to come back to worship with us."

"Oh, I will," Tony replied. "In fact, if you have time this week, I'd like to stop by and talk to you."

The pastor grinned as he pulled a card from his pocket and handed it to Tony. "Call my assistant and schedule an appointment. I look forward to getting to know you."

The crowd had thickened behind Tony, so he said good-bye and left. He found his car and headed to the condo he rented.

❧

Mandy spotted Tony chatting with the pastor right after church. She was all the way in the front, and it was packed, which made it impossible to get to him. She'd have to ask what he thought on Monday since that would be the next time they were both scheduled to work.

Pastor Waring patted her shoulder as she slipped past. "Thank you for inviting Tony. He seems like a nice fellow."

Mandy smiled. "Yes, he's very nice."

A slight smile quirked the pastor's lips. "Anything I need to know about?"

She quickly shook her head. "No, we're just friends. Well, not just friends, but—well, we work together. He's my boss."

The pastor nodded, still looking amused. "I understand. Have a good week, Mandy."

She couldn't get out of there fast enough. Once she reached her car, she let her head fall forward and rested it on her steering wheel. Why had such an innocent comment from the pastor gotten her all worked up? The second she questioned herself, she knew what the answer was. She was falling for Tony.

In spite of the fact that he got the job she wanted, and he kept a secret from her for so long, she knew his principles were solid. He not only talked about going to church and actually showed up, he apparently lived his faith—at least from what she'd seen so far. It didn't hurt that he was handsome, too.

How would she be able to face him now? Would she be able to hide her feelings, now that she was aware of them?

She'd have to. This *so* wasn't the time to let down her guard. He'd told her she was about to get a new position— one with more responsibility and she hoped a raise. This was what she'd been wanting.

But it would be nice to have a guy in her life. Brent from the electronics store used to flirt with her, but she had never been interested. However, Tony was a different matter.

Over the next week and a half, Mandy managed to avoid being in close quarters with Tony. When he was in his office, she stayed in the studio or at the front desk. When they had to communicate, she kept her comments brief but polite.

A few times she noticed that he looked puzzled, but she

didn't want to address that. Her job had to be first on her mind. Getting worked up over the boss wasn't good under any circumstances.

Tony hired a couple more part-timers to work at the counter—students who had no desire to be photographers or even have a career at Small World. They both admitted that they were short-timers, but at least they'd fill in the gap until some longer-term part-timers could be found. She appreciated the freedom to work in the studio without distractions.

≥

Tony had hoped that hiring a couple of extra people would ease things up for Mandy. She'd been so stressed lately, he worried about her. The way she avoided his gaze led him to believe something else might be going on.

Maybe telling her about the new career track hadn't been such a good idea. The last thing he wanted to do was put additional pressure on her.

After his appointment with Pastor Chuck, he knew he'd found the perfect church home—one where he'd be spiritually fed, he could get involved in some community outreach, and he'd find friends of like mind. The pastor was open and friendly, letting him know he was approachable. It was an excellent fit.

When Pastor Chuck asked about his relationship with Mandy, Tony had quickly let him know they were co-workers and that was all. The pastor nodded and changed the subject. Tony appreciated the lack of pressure.

He heard the buzzer at the door and glanced up in time to see Mandy walk into the studio. She lifted her hand and waved but then quickly glanced away.

"When you have a moment, I'd like to see you," he said.

"Sure," she replied. "Let me put my things down, and I'll be right there." In less than a minute, she was at the door of his office. "What's up?"

"Since you're leaving for Atlanta in the middle of the workday tomorrow, I can take you to the airport."

"You don't have to. I can get my sister to—"

"I'll take you." He cleared his throat. "That will be a good time for me to fill you in on some things you'll need to know—without the distractions here at the office."

She stood there for a moment before nodding. "Okay, that's fine. I'll have my sister take me to work, so I won't have to leave my car on the street."

"Good idea. Has she asked about the job?"

"Yes. Constantly. Any idea when we'll know something?"

Tony knew they'd been given the go-ahead to hire Christina, but he hesitated because he wasn't sure how Mandy felt about it. "Soon."

She smiled. "Fine. If you don't need me anymore, I have to set up the studio for my next appointment."

The rest of the day was business as usual. He went home after work and made a list of everything he needed to discuss with Mandy.

She came in early looking very professional in a business suit he'd never seen. His heart beat a little harder as he was reminded of how much he cared about what happened to her.

"You look nice," he said, trying his best to keep his tone professional.

She shuffled and blushed. "Thank you."

When it was time to go to the airport, they made sure the part-timers had everything under control. During the drive, Tony checked things off his list as he addressed them. "Just remember that you'll be asked your opinion, and you need to be open and honest."

"I wouldn't know how to be any other way," she said.

"Good." He pulled up to the departure section of the terminal and popped his trunk.

Once the curbside airline employee had her bag checked, she thanked him. "I appreciate everything you've done for me, Tony."

"It's my job. Call if you need anything."

"I will."

He sat and watched her as she disappeared into the building. The security person gestured for him to leave the curb, so he obeyed. All the way to the studio, he thought about how professional yet stunning Mandy looked. No doubt in his mind, the people in the home office would be as impressed as he was. And she clearly had no idea of the impact she had on people, which made her even more appealing.

Tony went straight back to work and relieved Steve, the part-time photographer who'd come in with the understanding he wouldn't have to stay long. A couple of hours later, the counter employee stuck her head into his office and said her shift was over, so she was leaving. He juggled photographing clients with walk-ins. This gave Tony a taste of what Mandy had dealt with over the past couple of months.

He'd finally finished up with the last proofs when the phone rang. It was Christina, sounding frantic.

"I've tried to call Mandy's cell phone, but it goes straight to voice mail."

"I'm sure she's okay," Tony said. "She probably just forgot to turn it on after her plane landed. Want me to give her a message?"

"Mom's in the hospital. She had a heart attack."

ten

Tony didn't waste a minute. As soon as he got the information, he called the Atlanta office. Uncle Ed's executive assistant, Tony's cousin Sharon, answered on the first ring.

"It's great to hear from you, Tony," she said. "Dad—"

"Is Mandy there yet?" he said.

"That's what I was trying to say. She's in with Dad." Her voice softened. "Why didn't you tell me how pretty she is?"

Tony cleared his throat. "I need to talk to her now."

"What's wrong, Tony?"

"Her mother had a heart attack. She'll need to come back right away."

"Hold on. Let me go get her."

"Wait. Sharon, why don't you get her and show her to the conference room—the one with the sofas? Then you can call me right back and put her on the phone."

"Good idea. I'll go do that now."

❧

Mr. Rossi had sent a stretch limo to the airport to pick Mandy up. And here she was, sitting in his office, listening to the details of a job better than she ever imagined.

Someone knocked on the door, and Mr. Rossi cleared his throat. "Yes?"

Sharon, the woman from the front desk, walked in and offered Mandy a sweet smile. "I need to see Mandy for a moment, if you don't mind."

"But we were—"

Sharon interrupted him. "It's important."

Mandy glanced over at the head of the company, who looked as perplexed as she felt. "Okay, if it's that important, go ahead. I'll be right here when you're done with her."

90

"Follow me," Sharon said. When they reached a room at the end of the long hall, she opened the door, switched on the light, and gestured inside. "Have a seat on the sofa over by the phone. I'll be right back, okay?"

"Um, sure," Mandy said, doing as she was told.

A moment later, Sharon was back. "Tony needs to talk to you, so let me get him on the phone." Without another word, she reached over, punched in the number, and handed the phone to Mandy. "I'll be out front when you're done."

"Tony?" Mandy said as soon as he answered. "What was so important to pull me out of my meeting?"

"Are you sitting down?" His voice was gravelly, unlike she'd ever heard it.

"Yes." Her heart suddenly started hammering in her chest. "What's going on?"

"Christina called. Your mother's in the hospital. She had a heart attack about an hour ago."

Mandy gasped. "I have to come home."

"I know. Sharon's booking your flight as we speak. I'll talk to my uncle and reschedule your meeting for later."

Within seconds after she hung up, Sharon was at the door of the conference room with her coat and handbag. "The driver is out front waiting. I'll ride with you to the airport."

"That's okay," Mandy said. "I'll be fine."

"I'm going with you," she insisted. "My dad's giving me the rest of the day off, so I can make sure everything's all set with the airline."

As Sharon coordinated the return trip, Mandy pulled out her cell phone, turned it on, and called her sister. "She's doing a little better," Christina said. "It was scary at first, though."

"Where was she?"

"In the kitchen," Christina said, her voice cracking. "I was arguing with her about needing to borrow her car, when she passed out." She let out a sob. "It's all my fault."

"It's not your fault," Mandy said.

"If I hadn't promised my friends I'd drive, none of this

would have happened. Ashley said she'd pick me up, but I told her I could use Mom's car."

"If you'd left, Mom might have passed out without you there to call the paramedics," Mandy reminded her.

"I didn't think about it like that. At any rate, I need to go back in the room. Dad's coming out, and I think he needs some coffee or something."

"Tell Mom I love her, and I'll be there soon."

After she clicked the OFF button, Mandy blinked. Her body was numb and she stared straight ahead.

As soon as the limo driver had all the bags and got into the driver's seat, Sharon took Mandy's hands. "Let's say a prayer."

Mandy bowed her head and listened to Sharon's soothing words of petition for her mother's healing and a safe trip back to West Virginia. When she opened her eyes, Mandy looked into Sharon's kind eyes.

"Thank you."

Sharon squeezed her hands. "Tony told us you were a Christian. Dad was relieved, since we like our management team to be of like mind. Faith in Christ has gotten my family through some trying times."

Mandy swallowed hard. "Yes, me, too."

To Mandy's surprise and relief, Sharon got out of the car, checked Mandy's bags at the curb, and walked her as far as she was allowed. She handed Mandy an envelope, leaned over, and gave her a hug. "We'll keep a prayer vigil going in the office. Let us know if there's anything we can do."

After Mandy found her gate, she opened the envelope and saw her boarding pass and a couple hundred dollars cash with a note to use it for incidentals. The folks at Small World were nicer and more generous than she ever realized before. Everywhere Mandy turned, she saw the Lord's gracious hand. Tears once again sprang to her eyes.

Lord, I pray that You spare my mother and show me how to let go of my need to make things like I want them. Your ways are so much greater than anything I'll ever think of on my own.

She opened her eyes, shoved the envelope into her purse, and pulled out her cell phone to call her dad. He explained that her mother's heart attack wasn't a complete surprise to him because she'd been having heart issues for a while. Mandy listened as he told her how her mom wanted to keep this a secret in order not to worry her and Christina. After she hung up, she sat there in stunned silence until she heard the announcement that her plane was ready for passengers.

Mandy was one of the last people to board, so she was stuck having to climb over the person who'd chosen the aisle seat in her row. But once she was buckled in, she closed her eyes and tried to shut out everything around her.

The flight was miserable as Mandy imagined all sorts of scenarios she might encounter when she got back. She prayed that her sister was right about their mom doing better.

After the plane arrived, and she walked out into the terminal, she saw Tony at the closest point security would allow. He extended a hand to take her carry-on bag then placed his hand in the small of her back to guide her toward baggage claim.

"I'll take you straight to the hospital," he said. "And I can stay as long as you need me."

"That's okay. You have a studio to run."

"It's covered." His tone was firm but kind. "Family has always come first with me, and I understand what you're going through."

Mandy didn't know what to say. However, she wondered what he meant by understanding what she was going through.

She didn't have to wait long to find out. Once they had her bags in the car, he opened up.

"Both of my parents have had health issues. My dad passed away when I was younger, but he'd been sick for a very long time. My mother broke down after he died, and she hasn't been the same since. Uncle Ed was the one who lifted the family. His faith kept him focused, and that's why I see the only way to true joy and contentment in life is through Christ."

"I had no idea," Mandy said softly. "I mean, I understand the part about faith in Christ, but I didn't know about your parents."

He offered a gentle smile. "There was no way for you to know until I told you. Now let's pray for your mom."

Mandy closed her eyes as Tony asked for strength for her family and healing for her mother. By the time he finished praying, any sliver of doubt she ever had about him had vanished. Tony was a true believer who genuinely cared about others.

Mandy studied Tony's profile as he drove. When he stopped for a red light, he turned and offered a sympathetic smile. "I'm sorry this is happening, but she's in very good hands."

"I know. Thank you for all you're doing."

"Would you like to hear some unrelated good news?"

Mandy nodded. "Yes, good news is always welcome."

"Everything checked out with Christina, and we can hire her. I just wanted to make sure you were one hundred percent okay with it."

"Why wouldn't I be?" The reservations Mandy had earlier had faded.

He shrugged. "I don't know. I just wanted to make sure you felt like she'd be a good fit for the office."

"She's good with people." Mandy thought back to one of the babysitting jobs they'd shared and how the little ones adored her sister. Deep down, Christina was a good person. Mandy now realized that part of her sister's immaturity had been caused by how the family had treated her. "Kids like her."

"That's important," he said.

Mandy turned back and faced the road as she thought about how much impact Tony had had on her life in such a short time. Her irritation over his sudden arrival had faded.

He pulled up in front of the hospital. "I'll let you out here.

After I park the car, I'll join you. Your mother's room is in the cardiac unit on the second floor." He touched her arm and looked at her with a tenderness that showed his sincerity.

"Thanks," she whispered as she got out.

◆

Tony thought about the irony of the situation. Mandy had to return home because her mother's heart was failing, and when he picked her up at the gate, just seeing her made his heart pump harder than a sprint.

He parked the car, jogged to the hospital entrance, and took the elevator to the second floor. The nurse on duty advised him that since he wasn't family, he couldn't go into Mrs. Pruitt's room. He knew that, so he was prepared to wait as long as it took for Mandy to visit with her mother.

Christina appeared a few minutes after he sat down. "Hey," she said. "Thanks for picking my sister up at the airport."

"No problem," he said. "I wanted to do it. So how's your mother doing?"

"Stable—at least for now." Christina's chin quivered. "When she dropped to the floor, I had no idea what was happening. I wish she'd told us she had a heart problem."

"She probably didn't want to worry her girls," Tony said. "I'm glad she's stable."

"I talked to the doctor about how I thought I might have caused her heart attack." Christina looked him in the eye as she paused. "He said the same thing you and Mandy did. It's a good thing I was there to call 911."

As silence fell between them, Tony noticed Christina fidgeting with anything she touched. She picked at a loose thread on her sleeve, then she peeled one of her fingernails. He decided to give her the news.

"Looks like we might have an offer for you soon," he said. "You did quite well on the test."

Her eyebrows went up. "I did?"

He nodded. "We have a few more things to do, but it looks good."

Christina's face lit up with a smile, then she slowly looked at the floor as the corners of her lips turned downward. "Does my sister know this?"

"Yes, she knows."

"And she doesn't mind?"

"Of course not. In fact, she pointed out that you're very good with children, which I'm sure you know is a plus."

She looked back up and into his eyes as a smile slowly spread over her lips. "Thank you, Tony. I'm sure this will be good for my mother's heart."

"Maybe," he said, "but don't take responsibility for causing her heart attack. I'm sure you had nothing to do with it."

"I guess we'll find out soon."

"Why don't we say a prayer?"

Christina swallowed hard then nodded. "Good idea."

They'd just lifted their heads when Mandy rounded the corner and joined them. Tony stood up. "How's she doing?"

"Mom seems to be in good spirits, considering all the tubes in her arms and machines everywhere." Mandy hugged Christina. "I'm so glad you were there, or she might not have made it."

Tony took a step back to give the sisters some space. He wanted to be there if needed but not get in the way.

When Mandy glanced in his direction, he felt his pulse quicken. "Would you mind taking me home so I can change clothes? Since Mom's resting, I figured this would be a good time."

"I'll be glad to," he said. He turned to Christina. "You have both of our cell phone numbers, right?"

She nodded. "If anything happens, I'll call right away."

❧

Mandy thanked Tony as he placed her bags by the door. "I should be able to come to work tomorrow if you need me."

"No. I made the schedule thinking you'd be at the home office, so you don't have to come in. You need to be with your family." He touched her cheek with the back of his hand but quickly pulled away. Mandy was again comforted by his presence and understanding of what she was going through.

After he left, she lowered her head and sent up a prayer of thanks—for her mother surviving the heart attack, for her sister being there, and for Tony's support. She changed out of her interview outfit and into more comfortable clothes. Then she made some sandwiches for her dad, her sister, and herself before heading for the hospital. On the way, she called her sister's cell phone.

"How's she doing?" she asked.

"She's napping right now," Christina said. "I'm worried about Dad. He's terribly distraught. I think he blames himself."

"I've been doing that, too," Mandy said. "We have to stop blaming ourselves. Instead, we should be thankful for the blessing of Mom surviving and getting the medical care she needs."

"They're planning to do an angioplasty soon. Oh, wait a minute. The doctor just came out, and he wants to talk to me."

"I'll be there in a few minutes."

After they hung up, Mandy focused on her driving. She wanted to hear what the doctor had to say, so once she found a parking spot, she ran to the hospital entrance. By the time she reached the second floor cardiac unit, she was out of breath. Fortunately, the doctor was still talking to her sister and dad.

The man in the white coat turned to her with a smile and extended his hand. "Dr. Jacobs," he said. "Your mother is fortunate to have had your sister right there with her. It was touch and go for a while, but I think we've got her stabilized enough with medications to do the procedure."

He explained how he planned to unblock a couple of her clogged arteries. "She'll be here for a week or so, depending on how well she does, and after she goes home, she'll need to take it easy for a while. Does she have someone there to take care of her?"

Mandy glanced at Christina, who nodded. Then she

thought about the job. "We both work for Small World Portrait Studio, so I think we can arrange our schedules to make sure someone is here at all times."

Christina's eyes widened, and she opened her mouth to say something. Mandy gestured for her to keep quiet for now.

eleven

After the doctor answered their questions, Christina turned to Mandy. "I got the job for sure?"

"I think so."

Christina settled back in her chair with a smile on her face. "Mom will be so happy about that. Now she and Dad won't have to worry about me, and I can find a place of my own so they can have peace and quiet again."

"Can you stay with them until Mom can get up and around again?" Mandy asked.

"Of course." Christina shook her head. "I'd never leave them stranded."

"I know." Mandy placed her hand on her sister's shoulder. "I'm so happy you're back. Everything is going to be just fine."

"I still feel like this is all my fault," Christina said.

"It's not your fault." Mandy gave Christina's shoulder a gentle squeeze.

"Thanks for trying to make me feel better, but I feel so guilty about arguing with her. If I had known. . ."

Mandy shook her head. "Mom hasn't felt good in years. On the way here, I talked to Dad and found out that she's been seeing a cardiologist since before you left. He recommended surgery a long time ago, but she was scared, so he prescribed some medication, hoping it would improve her condition."

"You're kidding. Why wouldn't she say anything?"

"She didn't want to worry us. Dad said she thought she had everything under control. Another thing is she didn't follow the diet the doctor put her on. That's going to change now."

"I had no idea." A bit of color returned to Christina's face.

"I'm glad you told me because I've been beating myself up over this."

"I know. But don't. Mom is in good hands now."

"I'll do everything I can to help her, including make her eat right."

Mandy smiled at her younger sister. "There's no doubt in my mind that you will."

"So how was your trip to Atlanta?"

It seemed like days since she'd been in Edward Rossi's office discussing her future with Small World. "I didn't have much time there, but Mr. Rossi had just told me that I'm being offered a promotion. I'll be the regional trainer for all new photographers."

Christina's face lit up. "Will you be my new boss?"

"No, but I'll probably teach you to work the equipment when you're ready. They're working on systems for new employees, and I don't think they've ironed everything out yet."

"I just hope I don't embarrass you."

Mandy felt a tug at her heart. "You've never embarrassed me, Christina. I'm proud of you, and I want to see you happy."

Christina was about to say something, when their dad appeared at the door, looking disheveled. Both sisters jumped up and ran over to him.

"How's she doing?" Mandy asked.

He raked his fingers through his hair. "She's stabilized, and they're getting her ready for surgery."

"Why don't we say a prayer?" Mandy said as she took hold of her sister's and dad's hands.

Mandy began, then their dad added his prayer. When he paused, Christina cleared her throat and said a few words. After they said "amen" Mandy fought back tears and squeezed her sister's hand before releasing it. She still had the desire to control everything, but at least she was aware of it. With the Lord's help, she'd continue to work on letting go.

"There's nothing we can do now but wait," Mandy said.

"Why don't we go on down to the cafeteria? I'll leave my cell phone number with the nurse, so she can call us if we're needed."

✧

Tony waited a couple of hours before calling Mandy to ask about her mom. He wanted to be there with her, but he didn't want to impose on her family while they stood vigil during Mrs. Pruitt's surgery. The employees at Small World obviously loved Mandy because as soon as he told them what had happened, everyone was concerned and offered to work more hours so she could be with her mother. Bella said she'd do whatever she could, and Steve offered to help with anything. He encouraged them all to pray.

After he felt like he'd waited long enough, Tony picked up the phone and punched in Mandy's cell phone number. She answered right away.

They had a short conversation. He told her everyone in the studio was praying for her family, and she gave him an update on her mom who had just gone into surgery.

After they hung up, he called his uncle in Atlanta. "Let us know if there's anything we can do," Uncle Ed said. "We've already ordered a card and fruit basket."

"Thanks. I'll keep you updated."

Tony went through the motions of making sure all the customers were taken care of, while the part-timers snapped shots of the children who came in. He kept watching the clock, wishing it would move faster so he could leave and go check on the Pruitt family.

Finally, it was time to say good-bye to his employees. After he got the night deposit together, he closed out the register and shut down the computer. They banked nearby, so all he had to do was walk a few doors down and drop the wallet in the night deposit box before leaving for the hospital.

He arrived shortly before ten o'clock and went straight up to the waiting area. Mandy was there with her dad, but Christina had left for the evening.

When Mandy looked up at him, she smiled. "Mom got out of surgery a few hours ago. Looks like everything will be fine."

Tony blew out a breath of relief. "I'm glad." He had to resist the urge to reach for her and pull her into an embrace, so he shuffled his feet and turned toward Mr. Pruitt. "You have two very strong daughters. I bet you and your wife are very proud of them."

Mr. Pruitt nodded. "They've always been good girls but a little spirited at times."

Mandy blushed, which Tony thought was sweet. "I'm sure I gave my parents plenty of. . .spirited behavior." He turned and winked at Mandy. She smiled.

"Thanks for giving Christina a position with your company," Mr. Pruitt said. "Once she learns what she needs to know, she'll do a good job."

"No doubt," Tony said. He wasn't sure if Mandy had mentioned her promotion yet, so he decided not to bring it up. "We've found that once we have an employee who exceeds expectations, other family members often do well, too."

"To be honest, I was a little surprised you didn't have an antinepotism policy. But her mother and I are very happy."

⁂

Mandy touched her dad's arm. "You told her already?"

Her dad nodded. "After she came to, her first question was how you and Christina were holding up. I told her you flew back from an important meeting to be with her, and Christina got a good job with your company. That made her happy."

"Good," Tony said. "Looks like everything will be just fine. If there's anything I can do for any of you, let me know, okay?" He paused as his gaze met Mandy's. "Take the time you need. You haven't used any of your paid time off, and if you need more, I'll see what I can do."

"Thanks, Tony."

"I better go." Tony extended his hand to Mandy's dad.

After they shook, he hesitated before reaching for her hand. As his grip tightened on hers, she felt an odd sensation fluttering around in her stomach. He quickly let go and shoved his hand into his pocket. "Call me tomorrow if you have time." Then he turned and left.

After he turned the corner, Mandy's dad stepped up beside her and put his arm around her. "Your boss seems to be a good man."

Mandy nodded. "Yes, he really is."

"Ya know, back in my day, portrait studios were run by people who studied a long time to become photographers. I have to admit I'm surprised he wanted to hire Christina."

"I didn't have photography experience when they hired me, remember?"

"Yeah, seems I do remember, but somehow you never surprise me. You've always succeeded at everything."

"Not everything."

"Pretty near everything. How will your sister know how to take pictures? She's always been in front of the camera, not behind it."

"We have great equipment that's easy to use with the right training. My new job will be to teach people how to operate the equipment and what to do to get the best shots of children."

"That's good. I hope she catches on fast."

"She will." Mandy slipped her arm in his and kissed his cheek. "She has good genes."

"So tell me more about Tony. Is he single?"

"Da—ad." Mandy laughed. "I can't believe you just asked me that."

"You can't blame me for looking out after my two daughters." He tilted his head and looked at her from beneath his heavy eyebrows. "My two *available* daughters. I want you and your sister to be happy and have fulfilling lives."

"I can't speak for Christina, but I don't need a man in my life to be fulfilled."

"I know, but it's always nice to have someone to share your experiences with."

Mandy couldn't argue that point. She had to admit, if only to herself, she'd experienced some loneliness. There were times even Brent from the electronics store from across the street seemed appealing. Then she came to her senses.

"If some nice young man just happens to cross your path, I hope you at least consider getting to know him."

"Okay, Dad, I promise I'll give someone a chance—as long as he's a Christian man."

"That goes without saying." He glanced at his watch. "I wonder how your mother's doing."

"Why don't we go see?"

❧

The next morning, Tony arrived at the studio and was surprised to see Mandy there. "Why aren't you at the hospital with your mom?"

"She's doing much better, and I thought it would be better to take time off after she gets home."

"Excellent point." Tony had scheduled around Mandy, figuring she'd need at least a week or two. "Let me call the part-timers and let them know they don't have to come in."

After he finished calling people, he came back out to the reception area and saw Mandy looking over the schedule. "Looks like we'll be busy today. Good." She came around the counter, straightened up some of the displays on the table, then walked toward the studio before she stopped and turned to face him. "When do you think Christina will be able to start?"

"I have the paperwork in my office. When do you think she'd like to start?"

"As soon as possible. I think she's excited about working here."

"By the way, my uncle said he'd like to talk to you. He's planning a trip here so you won't have to go back to Atlanta. He's bringing his wife and making a little vacation of it, so I thought maybe you could give them some ideas of things to do while they're here. I thought he might want to stay at Oglebay Park in the Wilson Lodge."

"Sounds like a nice vacation. Does he play golf?"

"He loves it. My aunt will have to find something to do while he's working, though." He thought for a minute then added, "You'll like my aunt."

"I'm sure I will." Mandy smiled. "Your whole family has been nice to me."

"Maybe you can show her around one afternoon—that is, if your mother is doing okay, and you have time."

His heart warmed at the smile that spread over her face. "I'd love to. Just let me know when," she said softly before disappearing into the studio.

Tony did his paperwork then stuck his head in the studio. Mandy glanced up. "Need something?"

"I'd like to have Christina come in sometime tomorrow if she's available."

"Want me to call her?" she asked.

"If you want. Or I can."

She pulled her bottom lip between her teeth as she thought about it, then she smiled. "Why don't you call her? It'll mean more since you'll be her supervisor."

Mandy finished setting up the photography area then went back to the counter to make some calls. She wanted to stay as busy as possible while at work to keep from thinking about her mother. She knew Tony would understand if she needed to drop everything if her family needed her. As long as her mother was still in the hospital, Mandy could visit without having to worry too much.

Tony appeared at the end of the counter about fifteen minutes later. "I had a nice conversation with Christina. She's excited about working here, but I understand that she's needed at home, so I told her she could start whenever she wanted to. She wants to start as soon as possible, so I told her she could come in now or wait until after your mother was settled."

"What did she say?"

"I'm waiting for her to call me back. She said she needed to talk to your dad and the doctor."

Mandy was impressed. Her sister had obviously been jolted into another burst of maturity. "Since I'll be doing the photography training, I'll have to be here with her."

"That's another thing I wanted to discuss with you. We're hiring her into the management training program. One of the things they're working on at the home office is a manual with self-administered tests. I'll work with her on company systems and some management policies. After we get past the first part of the training, which should last a couple of weeks, I'll turn her over to you. We haven't done the photographers' manual yet, and we'd like for you to be involved."

Mandy's ego jumped up a couple of notches. "Thanks, Tony."

"I mean it. You have skills that we need to teach others. I just hope we choose the right people who are willing to learn."

"It's really not all that hard." She'd never gotten so many compliments in her life.

"It took me three weeks to master the camera and poses," Tony said. "How long do you think it'll take someone like your sister who doesn't have much experience with a camera?"

She looked pensive for a minute as she stuck a card back in the file drawer. "There's more than just learning the camera and poses. I'll want to work with her on behavior modification for the kids who are—well, rather difficult."

Tony grinned. "She couldn't have a better teacher."

Mandy felt her face heat up. "I remember what it's like to be a kid wearing miserable clothes and being told to sit still when I wanted to get up and run."

"Yeah, I remember that, too." He chuckled. "I think most people forget what it's like to be a child."

"Probably." She finished her filing, pushed the drawer shut then turned to face Tony. As soon as their eyes made contact, she felt a giant thud in her chest.

He blinked and took a step back. Had he felt it, too?

❧

Tony felt like he'd been hit head-on by a tidal wave. The warmth of Mandy's hazel eyes with the gold flecks caused a sensation unlike anything he'd ever experienced.

He cleared his throat and shuffled his feet. "Um. . .when your sister comes in, I'll get her started on the training manual. I think we'll have a better idea of when she's ready for you after she gets started."

She slowly nodded. "I think that's wise."

He remembered his new hire was due in a couple of hours. "While you were out, I went ahead and hired a new part-time photographer. I wasn't sure if you'd be back so soon, so I told her I'd work with her until our crackerjack photographer returned."

"Crackerjack, huh?" She looked amused.

"Well, you're much more than that."

Her smile widened. "Thanks."

Tony was relieved when the phone rang. He gestured toward it. "Want me to get that?"

"No, I've got it." She lifted the receiver and gave him one last smile before she turned her full attention to the caller.

Tony went back to his office to get the paperwork ready for the new photographer to sign. His cousin had encouraged him to get to know Mandy better outside of work, and he understood why. He had no doubt that they'd make a great team—both at work and as friends, or more. When Mandy appeared at the door, he motioned for her to come inside.

As soon as she did, he leaned forward. "How would you like to go out to lunch after church on Sunday?"

twelve

Mandy's heart rate doubled. Had Tony just asked her out on a date?

He held up his hands. "Don't feel like you have to. It's not like a date or anything."

Okay, so it wasn't a date. "That would be nice."

"I haven't been in town long enough to know the best places. Any suggestions?"

Mandy didn't normally go out to lunch on Sundays, so she wasn't sure. She shrugged. "What kind of food do you like?"

"Anything I don't have to cook," he replied. "We can decide then."

"Sounds good."

Tony put down his pen, leaned back, and folded his arms. "Okay, so what do you need?"

She tilted her head. "Um. . ."

"You came in here, remember?"

Mandy shuffled her feet as she tried to remember what she wanted. "Must not have been very important."

"If you remember, you know where I am." She started to turn and leave, but he called her name. "I almost forgot to tell you, we're planning a regional campaign that should start in about three months."

"What kind of campaign?"

"TV, radio, newspaper, and magazine ads. We've been working on it for a while, and we about have everything nailed down."

"Anything I can do to help?" Mandy asked.

"Yes, as a matter of fact, everyone on the management team will be asked to look over the package before it goes out."

Management team. That sounded nice. "I'm sure it'll be good."

"The biggest holdup is getting the actors for the TV ads.

Ricco isn't happy with what they've done."

"How about using real people?"

"Real people?" he asked. "Like customers?"

Mandy nodded. "Yes. I can think of several customers who'd love to be involved in something like this."

"Not a bad idea. Let me run it past Ricco and see what he thinks. The kids they've filmed are already overexposed, and we're concerned about the credibility of using them, so I think he just might go for it."

"You know my sister went to Hollywood to be an actress," Mandy reminded him.

"Yes, I know." He pursed his lips. "But I'm not sure it would be such a good idea to have her in a TV ad just yet. We need her to focus on her job here and not see this as a stepping-stone back to where she wanted to go."

"If you want me to talk to her about that, I will," Mandy offered.

The buzzer on the door sounded, alerting them that someone had entered. "It's up to you," Tony said.

ϟ

The next several days, Mandy spent most of her time either at the studio or with her mother at the hospital. Each day seemed to be better than the one before.

"The doctor says I can go home Monday," her mother said when Mandy entered the room on Saturday. "Would you mind helping Christina get rid of all the unhealthy food? I'm afraid I won't be able to resist it if it's there."

Mandy laughed as she patted her tummy. "Oh, I'll get rid of it."

"Please eat healthy," her mother said. "I don't want you to wind up like me. Between the high-fat food and worry, I'm afraid I've been a bad example."

Mandy stroked her mother's hair. "You've been a wonderful mother. But you do need to stop worrying about Christina and me. We're adults now. You've done your job."

"I know." Her mother smiled and reached up to take

Mandy's hand. "It's just so hard, though, to turn off what I've been doing for twenty-some years."

"Now that Christina has a job, there's nothing left to worry about. She said she wants to live with you and Dad for a while so she can help out until you get your health back. And you know where I am."

Her mother nodded and smiled as tears sprang to her eyes. "I'm so blessed."

"Our whole family is," Mandy said.

"I'm glad Christina's back. When she left, I felt like my heart would break in two."

Mandy stilled as she remembered Christina expressing guilt over causing their mother's heart attack. "Did you tell her that?"

"I was so upset, I probably did." A stricken look came over her face. "You don't think she's blaming herself for what happened to me, do you?"

Bingo. "Don't worry about that now. Just do whatever it takes to get better. But no more health secrets, okay?"

Her mother nodded. "I'll talk to her."

Mandy gave her another hug. "I have to go to work today, but Tony's encouraging me to take some time off to spend with you."

"I don't want you to risk your job for me."

"Don't be silly, Mom. I wouldn't want to work for a company where they didn't value family."

Her mother smiled. "Christina says Tony's a very sweet man."

Mandy felt heat rise to her cheeks as her mother studied her. "He is nice."

"So do you like him?"

"He's a very good boss."

"You know what I mean, Mandy. Christina thinks he's interested in you."

Mandy tried hard not to smile. "Don't pay any attention to that. He's a very nice, caring boss who knows he needs to treat his employees well to keep them happy."

"I don't want you missing out on an opportunity to find love, Mandy. Even if he is your boss."

Mandy forced a laugh. "That's just it. Because he's my boss, I need to respect him as my supervisor. Period."

"Okay, okay, I hear you. Just don't ever put a job ahead of true love."

"I love you, Mom." Mandy bent over to kiss her mother on the cheek then backed away. "If you need me, just call or tell Dad to call me, and I'll be here."

Her mother lifted a hand and wiggled her fingers in a wave before turning to face the window on the other side of the room. Mandy left the hospital room and nearly collided with her sister as she rounded the corner to the elevator.

"How's Mom?" Christina asked.

Mandy grabbed her sister by the arm and steered her toward the waiting area. "I want to make sure you understand that you had nothing to do with Mom's heart attack."

"What made you say that?"

"She said she told you that her heart would break if you left. You do realize that's a figure of speech, right?"

Christina's shoulders sagged as she expelled a breath. "I don't know. It seems like everything I've ever done has upset Mom and Dad. Back in high school, when I made cheerleader, Mom got frustrated over my uniform."

"That's because you didn't tell her you needed it until the weekend before the first game."

"She should have figured it out, since I made the squad. Then there was the play when I needed to color my hair purple."

Mandy laughed at the memory. "Well, I have to admit, it did look permanent. You should have told us you were doing a temporary rinse."

"See?" Christina lifted her hands then dropped them, slapping her sides. "You would have known all that stuff. I've just been such a loser all my life."

"You are not a loser. You've had so many things going on,

you forgot to communicate." Mandy put her arm around Christina and hugged her. "You were very busy back in high school, but that was then. Now you're all grown up, and you're about to start a wonderful career."

"What if I mess up on the job?" Christina asked. "It'll be hard if they expect me to measure up to you."

"Don't worry about that. Tony's a very smart man who knows we're two separate, very different people."

"I hope so. I sure don't want to disappoint another person."

Mandy gently turned her sister toward their mother's hospital room and gave her a little push. "Go see Mom. I have to go to work so I can relieve you next week. Tony's been working on a training program for you."

"I'll try to make you proud, Mandy." Her eyebrows went up as she reached into her pocket and pulled out an envelope. "Oh, I almost forgot. I went to a consignment shop, and they sold some of my LA clothes that I couldn't use here, and now I can pay you back for the plane ticket."

"You don't have to pay me right now if you need the money for new clothes," Mandy said.

Christina firmly handed it to her. "Yes, I do. It's part of my growing up and taking responsibility."

Mandy thought about her need to let go and stop trying to mother her sister. She put the envelope into her purse. "Thank you, Christina. I'm really proud of you."

❧

Tony had just walked out of the back part of the studio when Mandy walked in. "How's your mom?"

"She's doing much better. They're releasing her on Monday."

"Good. I'll call Steve to come in." As he talked, he noticed Mandy's look of concern. "What's wrong?"

"Nothing." She cleared her throat.

He'd been around her enough to know better. "If you need to talk, I'm all ears. I might not know how to fix whatever the problem is, but I can at least listen."

"Thanks." Mandy headed off down the hall to the office

where she kept her handbag then came out, brushing her hands together. "I'm ready to work."

He chuckled. "I can tell." He started to go into his office, until he heard her clear her throat, so he turned around to see her looking at him.

"Tony?"

"Yes?" As they held their gaze, everything else around them seemed insignificant. "Did you need something?"

"Thank you for hiring my sister."

Tony sat back as she paused. "You don't have to thank me."

"No one realized how smart she was, but I knew. It's not that easy being so popular and juggling such a busy schedule."

"I can imagine," Tony said. "Somehow you did just fine."

"We hung out in different circles. Mom and Dad always thought of her as the fragile sister, while I was sturdy and capable. Then when she informed us that she was leaving for Hollywood without a single prospect for a job, Mom and Dad hit the roof."

"Must have been rough on them." He'd already figured most of this out, but Mandy obviously needed to talk.

Mandy nodded. "Oh, it was very rough. They called me every day after she first left, wondering if I'd heard from her. Most of the time, I hadn't. So I started calling her. She was always in a hurry and needed to go."

Tony nodded. "I remember being her age—too busy for people who cared the most. But I bet you never felt that way."

"I did, but I never had the nerve to act on it or say what Christina said." She paused. "When she finally called and said she was stranded, I have to admit I was annoyed."

"Understandable."

"But I wasn't about to leave her in a lurch. I had some hard feelings about her expecting everyone to drop everything, but once she got home, I realized that was my problem, not hers. She was just finished testing her wings, and now she was ready to come home."

"So how do you feel about her working here?"

"That's what I'm getting at. I have no doubt my sister can do a fabulous job, once she gets into it."

"With you as her trainer, she'll be an excellent photographer."

Mandy smiled. "Thank you. I hope you're right."

"Don't sell yourself short, Mandy," Tony said. "You're an amazing woman."

He waited for her to say something, but she just stood there.

"I appreciate you telling me all this. I know how difficult it must have been for you."

"It was extremely hard," she agreed as she stood. "I need to set up the studio for my next customers now."

After she left the office, Tony prayed that he'd be able to do whatever it took to bring out the best in both of the Pruitt sisters.

At the end of the busy afternoon, Mandy stopped by his office, where he was putting the final changes in Christina's training manual. "Thanks for listening, Tony. I wanted to make sure you understood that my sister and I are completely different."

"You made your point, but I already figured that out." And he admired Mandy now, more than ever.

"Thanks."

Tony shut down the computer, while Mandy got her personal belongings from the other office. They met in the reception area as they were about to leave for the day.

"Wanna do something tonight?"

She stopped and turned to face him. "Do something?"

He lifted a shoulder and tried to appear casual. "Yeah, like go out or—I don't know—eat dinner and maybe take in a movie."

The slow smile that spread across her face warmed his heart. "Yes, I'd like that."

"I'll pick you up in an hour, okay?"

"Sounds good."

૨ફ

The evening was delightful and would have been even better if

Tony had gotten the nerve to kiss her good night at her door. But instead, he stood there, shuffling his feet, telling her how much he appreciated working with her. This was the first time in his life he hadn't known what to say to a woman he cared about. But it was also his first time to go out with someone he worked with. Finally, he just reached up and squeezed her shoulder.

"I had a nice time," she said, her voice barely above a whisper.

"Want me to pick you up for church in the morning?"

She looked directly up at him and nodded. "Sure."

❧

The next morning, Mandy stared straight ahead as the pastor delivered his sermon. Her sister sat on one side of her, and Tony was on the other side. It felt right.

Tony escorted both of them to the parking lot, where he turned to Christina. "Mandy and I are going to lunch. Would you like to join us?"

Christina lifted an eyebrow and glanced back and forth between them then grinned and slowly shook her head. "Nah, I don't think so. I'll go hang out at the hospital and give Dad a break."

"We won't be long," Mandy said quickly. "As soon as I get back, I'll join you."

Christina touched Mandy's arm and snorted. "No, go have some fun. Your work will be cut out for you once I start at Small World."

On their way to the car, Tony leaned over and whispered, "Your sister is very smart and funny."

Mandy nodded. "Where are we going?"

"I wanted to go to Figaretti's, but they don't open until four. Where would you like to eat?"

"Why don't we go across the bridge to Ohio Valley Mall? I'm sure we'll find something there."

"Great idea. We've been thinking about putting a studio in that mall, so I can check it out."

thirteen

Mandy got to the studio before anyone else on Monday morning. She promised her dad and sister she'd be at the hospital when her mother was released at ten o'clock, but she wanted to make sure everything she'd scheduled at work was in order.

Tony arrived fifteen minutes later. "I didn't think you were coming in today."

"The Phillips twins have the first appointment, and they're rather difficult." She arranged some of the props on the table by the camera. "Jonathan likes the monkey, and Jason always tries to take it away from him, even though he's more interested in the model cars." She held one up to demonstrate her point.

"Mandy!" Tony crossed the room and took the model car from her then set it down on the table.

"Sorry. I know you can handle them. It's just that—well, I don't want anyone to struggle."

"I know you don't." Tony pointed to the stool behind her, then he pulled one up and sat down. "Listen. You're going into management soon, and that means you'll have to delegate. If you try to do it all yourself, you'll go crazy, not to mention the fact that you'll wind up building weakness in your trainees."

She pondered that for a moment. "I didn't think about it that way."

"I understand. In fact, when I read over the management training stuff for Uncle Edward, I realized how important it was to back away at some point and let people practice what you taught them."

Mandy knew he was right. "Okay, here's my bag of tricks. If

116

one toy doesn't work, try another until you hit on something that keeps the kids' attention."

He laughed and stood up. "Attagirl. Now go help your family. If you need me, I'll be glad to do what I can. Steve will be here around noon, and Bella said she's ready to take on more hours."

"Thanks, Tony." She started toward the door then stopped. "Oh, I almost forgot. Christina said she could start this afternoon if you want her to."

"I think tomorrow morning will be soon enough. I'll have all her books ready in the office. The first thing I want to teach her is how to answer the phone and deal with walk-ins."

Mandy turned to leave but stopped and smiled at Tony. "Thanks for lunch yesterday. I had fun."

"Me, too," he said. "I think Ohio Valley Mall is the perfect place for a Small World Portrait Studio. In fact, we're considering relocating this one if the rent keeps going up on Market Street."

"I'd hate to shut this place down."

"But then again, we might not. We like it here, too, and you've built a nice base of steady customers."

"Good. I guess it's time to go now."

Tony laughed. "Yes, I guess it is. Now scoot."

When Mandy arrived at the hospital, she headed straight for the elevator. The door opened on the second floor, and she saw her sister and dad standing outside her mother's room, talking.

"What's going on?" she asked as she approached them.

"The doctor got here early," her dad said. "They're getting her ready to leave, so we should be out of here in a few minutes."

Mandy let out a sigh of relief. Her sister arched an eyebrow and gave her a once-over. "Are you okay?"

"Sure, I'm fine." Mandy self-consciously ran her hands down the front of her blouse and pants. "Why?"

"You just look—well, different." Christina tilted her head and grinned.

"Hey, y'all, they're letting me go home. Finally!"

All heads turned to Mandy's mother as the nursing assistant wheeled her out of the room. "I'll wheel her down to the lobby. If you can pull your car up to the loading area, I'll help her in."

Mandy and Christina stayed behind while their dad went to get the car. Their mother wore a huge smile. "I can't believe I'm finally able to go home and sleep in my own bed."

"Don't you like the service here?" the assistant teased.

"It's great if you like getting prodded, pinched, and awakened at all hours of the day and night." She snorted. "The night nurse woke me up to see if I needed a sleeping pill."

Mandy laughed. "It can't be that bad."

"You're right," her mother agreed. "But I do miss my own bed."

Christina winked at Mandy. "I went through the cupboards and fridge and got rid of all the cookies, ice cream, and other unhealthy foods, just like you told me to."

Their mother groaned. "Looks like I'll have some adjusting to do, but at least I have someone to help me through it."

By the time they got her home, she was out of breath. "Easy does it," their dad said as he lifted her and carefully placed her on the sofa.

"I'm not an invalid," she said. "I can walk."

"I know," he replied. "But let me spoil you a little bit. It makes me feel good."

Christina nudged Mandy toward the kitchen. "We'll fix you something yummy and healthy to eat. Be right back."

Once they reached the kitchen, Christina leaned against the counter and chuckled softly, with her hand over her mouth. "Dad was so worried, and now he's treating her like fragile glass. I never realized how lost he'd be without her until this."

Mandy nodded. "Sometimes it takes a scare to snap people's attention back to where it should be."

"You got that right. This whole thing reminded me how

important it is to lean on the Lord. I never stopped believing, but I have to admit there were times when I didn't think about His hand in my life."

"I know exactly what you're saying," Mandy admitted. "He's shown me that I can't control everything around me."

Christina smiled. "I guess we'll always be works in progress."

They worked on a vegetable platter with the produce Christina had bought. She held up a small container of low-fat yogurt. "I have a great recipe for dip that is actually heart healthy."

"Great! I could use some of that myself. I think this is a wake-up call for all of us."

"Ya know, I've never had my cholesterol checked," Christina said as she dumped the ingredients into a bowl and stirred. "Mom isn't overweight, so I assumed she was healthy. Who would have thought she had cholesterol as high as hers?"

"I know. I think all of us will be healthier now." Mandy plunged a stick of celery into the yogurt dip then tasted it. "Yum. That's delicious. In fact, I think I like that better than the high-fat stuff we used to eat."

Christina picked up a cookbook and showed it to Mandy. "I found this heart-healthy cookbook with easy recipes, so I don't think this will be too hard. Dad and I have been experimenting with a few things so we'd at least have something to fix for Mom when she got home."

"You're kidding. You got Dad in the kitchen?"

With a nod, Christina chuckled. "Yeah, can you believe it?"

"Now I know he must have been scared."

They fixed some iced decaf green tea and put everything on a tray that Christina carried out to their parents. "Here's a snack to enjoy while Mandy and I fix lunch."

By the time Mandy went back to her own place that night, she was certain that her sister had everything under control. To Mandy's amazement, Christina had a week's worth of menus and exercises lined up for their mom. And even more surprising, their mom seemed perfectly content following orders.

The next morning, when Mandy arrived back at her parents' house to relieve her sister, her dad said Christina had already left for work. "She was pacing and acting all nervous," he explained. "I figured we'd all be better off if she went on over there."

"You're probably right. How was Mom's night?"

"She was a little restless, and I couldn't sleep, so we spent about an hour talking."

"Doesn't she need sleep?"

"Yes, but I think it was good to get everything out."

"Are y'all talking about me?"

Mandy and her dad looked up to see her mother standing in the doorway of the living room. She was dressed in a jogging suit and had her makeup on.

"You look nice, Mom," Mandy said as she crossed over to give her a hug. "Are you planning to go out?"

"Maybe a walk around the block." She cut her gaze over to her husband before adding, "I need to work up to a couple of miles soon, but I figure the block is all I can handle just yet."

"What can I do?" Mandy asked.

"Wanna go for a walk with us?"

"Sure, Mom. Let me go out to my car and get my sneakers. I'll be right back."

Mandy was pleased that her mother was willing to do whatever it took to get healthy. That meant everyone's life would get back to normal more quickly. She spent the remainder of the day helping and watching her dad cater to her mother's whims.

Christina came home at dinnertime. "I am exhausted," she said as she dropped onto the sofa. "There is so much to learn, I feel like my head is swollen ten times its normal size."

Mandy took a step back and studied her head. "Nope. No swelling that I can see."

"How long did it take you to learn how to do all that stuff?"

"Not long. And I didn't have a manual. I'm glad they have

some training materials now. It'll be so much easier if you can look stuff up."

Christina's face suddenly lit up as she straightened. "Tony said I can actually start working tomorrow, since I spent the whole day studying."

"Working?" Mandy asked. "As in taking pictures?"

"Ya know. . ." Christina tapped her chin with her index finger. "I'm not sure what I'll be doing. All I know is I'll be glad to move around a little. My back is killing me from sitting all day."

"Dinner's ready. Mom is in the kitchen right now. She and Dad have gone for two walks around the block. She's gradually working up to her two miles per day."

"Looks like we're all learning new stuff." Christina stood up and stretched.

"God has a way of making us learn what He wants us to know."

Christina frowned. "You don't think God actually caused Mom's heart attack, do you?"

"I don't think so. But I do think He's using it to bring all of us closer and showing us how fortunate we are."

After dinner, Mandy went back to her place. Her parents asked if they could be alone the next day, so she called Tony's cell phone to let him know she wanted to work.

"That's fine with me. At least they're not far, so if you're needed, you can be there in a few minutes."

Mandy arrived early on Wednesday, then Tony followed. Christina walked in five minutes before they opened.

Grinning, she looked at Tony. "You said I could start working. What do you want me to do?"

"Remember the phone section in the manual? I'd like for you to answer calls and receive walk-ins." He handed her a stack of cards. "Between calls, you can file these prospect cards. After you're comfortable with the reception area, I'll teach you how to follow up on some of those folks who have called or expressed interest in having portraits done."

Christina frowned but took the cards. Mandy knew her sister was unhappy, but she needed to get over it. So Mandy left the front desk and went into the studio, where everything had been neatly put away.

"I tried to leave it like you do," Tony said from behind her. "Does it pass inspection?"

Mandy spun around to face him, and she lost her breath when she realized he was less than two feet away. "Yes." Her throat tightened. "It looks very nice."

He closed the distance between them and took her hands. "Mandy, I—"

"Excuse me," Christina said from the door. "I have a question."

Tony took a quick step back and turned toward the door. "What do you need?"

"How long do I have to stand at the front desk? I have all the cards filed, and no one has walked in yet."

Mandy glanced up at the big clock on the studio wall. They'd been there for less than half an hour, and her sister was already bored. She started say something, but she held back. This was Tony's deal. He needed to handle the situation as he would for any trainee.

"Would you rather go back to the office and study some more?" he asked.

"Um. . ." Christina glared at Mandy, but Mandy looked away. "Would it be okay if I brought my study materials up to the front desk? At least I'd have something to do when I'm not talking on the phone."

"Sure, that would be just fine," Tony replied. "Just remember the customer always comes first."

"I know that." Christina turned and left them alone again.

When Tony looked at Mandy again, she had to hold back the grin that threatened. His shoulders shook with silent laughter. "I can't say you didn't warn me."

"I never said anything about what she just did."

"No, but I'm good at reading between the lines. Your

sister is sharp, and she needs to be constantly challenged. I'm thinking we might speed her through the management material in the book and move her into some photography a little sooner than originally planned. Are you up to that?"

"Of course," she replied. "I'll do whatever I need to do."

"Do you realize how much more walk-in traffic we'd get in the mall?"

Mandy reluctantly nodded. "I suppose we probably would."

"Right now, our rent is much lower than mall rent, but the paperwork for renewing our lease just came in this morning, and it's worse than we thought. Ricco said it's sky-high—close to mall rent, and they're not budging because other businesses want this space."

"When do we have to sign the lease?" Mandy asked.

"The current lease is up in six months, but I think we have another ninety days on a month-to-month."

Nine months. At least they had that long before they had to move. Besides, it wasn't like they'd be going far. Ohio Valley Mall was just on the other side of the bridge. Fifteen minutes away. But still. . .

"We'd need to assess other aspects besides the rent, though. Like I already said, we have a solid base of customers, and we need to see if they're willing to go to the mall. If not, we need to evaluate cost versus income—or at least potential income."

"Mandy," Christina hollered from the front. "I need you."

"Sorry," Mandy said as she ran toward the front. "I'll have a talk with her after work."

fourteen

Mandy braced herself to face her sister. "Whatcha need?"

Christina glared at her. "You never told me how boring this job was. I hate standing here, waiting for nothing to happen."

"Then don't just stand there," Mandy said. "Be proactive. Study your materials."

"I've studied them until my brains felt like they'd implode. Is this what you do all day?"

Mandy thought for a moment then gestured toward a stool. "Have a seat, Christina. We need to talk about this whole situation."

Christina did as she was told and sat. "Okay, now what?"

"Small World is currently in a transition. Until recently, there were no training manuals. People got hired and trained on the job. They were thrown into a situation, and they had to swim, or they'd sink fast."

"You did just fine with that."

"Not really." Mandy thought about how in the dark she'd been since she'd started. "Once I started working here, I was determined to make it work. I enjoy taking pictures of the children, so I focused on learning everything I could about how to do the best job at it."

"Why can't I do that?"

Mandy took her sister's hand. "You can. But don't expect this to be an exciting job right off the bat. Tony already mentioned that we need to speed things up a bit with you, and once we do that, brace yourself."

A myriad of expressions crossed Christina's face, from consternation to contemplation and then satisfaction. "Okay, I think that'll be good. I understand everything so far, so there's really no reason I can't jump into the next step."

"Okay. Perhaps Tony will let you come back and observe the picture-taking process. We'll have to have someone at the desk, though."

Christina seemed satisfied with that. "Thanks, Mandy. I'm glad I have you going to bat for me."

"I don't mind doing it now, but I won't always be here to deal with stuff like this."

Suddenly, a look of panic shot across Christina's face. "You won't?"

"No, because I'll be traveling after I start the training."

"Oh." Christina frowned. "I guess I'm your guinea pig, huh?"

Mandy laughed. "Yes, but a very cute guinea pig."

Tony walked up with his hands in his pockets. "Are you two okay?"

"Christina would like to move a little faster in her training, and I think she's ready for the next step."

"I agree." Tony looked at Christina. "We don't have the photography training nailed down yet, but I think Mandy will know what to do."

Mandy nodded. "I'd also like to teach her to call prospects who requested more information. She doesn't like standing here waiting for walk-ins."

"Did you tell her about the mall?"

Mandy shook her head. "I didn't know if I should say anything."

Tony turned to Christina. "We've been looking at moving to the Ohio Valley Mall."

She crinkled her forehead. "We are? Why?"

He explained the rent situation. "Sometimes it just comes down to economics."

Christina pondered what he said for a moment then her eyes lit up. "Cool! I love the mall!"

"I know you do," Mandy said as she and Tony exchanged an amused glance.

"I can go shopping at lunch and maybe even get my nails done at the salon."

Mandy groaned. "You'll just need to put yourself on a budget, so you don't spend your whole check in the other stores."

Tony chuckled as he walked away. "I'll leave you two to work this out. But do whatever you think about the photography training, Mandy."

After he closed his office door, Christina made a face. "Am I annoying him?"

Mandy shook her head. "I doubt it. He's just really busy with all the changes."

"Okay, so what should I do next?" Christina hopped off the stool and walked back to the front part of the counter.

"Have you gotten to the section in the manual where it tells how to contact people from the mail-in forms?"

Christina nodded and scrunched her nose. "I hate phone solicitation."

"It's not really phone solicitation since they filled out the forms and requested information. All you have to do is call, tell them you're available for any questions, and invite them in. Make sure you have a price list nearby because a lot of people want prices."

"It's okay if I quote prices over the phone?"

Mandy tilted her head. "Of course. Why wouldn't it be?"

Christina hung her head. "I guess I must not have told you that I worked as a phone solicitor for a company in Hollywood that wouldn't allow us to mention price. I hated that job."

"You definitely didn't tell me about that. How long did you work there?"

"About three hours. After getting hang-up after hang-up, I finally just grabbed my handbag, marched right into my supervisor's stuffy office, and told him I quit." She frowned. "He had the nerve to laugh right in my face. He said I'd never amount to anything."

An alarm sounded in the back of Mandy's mind, but she tried to squelch it. "You've been with Small World longer than that." She pointed to the date on the calendar. "It must not be too bad here."

The color in Christina's face drained, and she grabbed Mandy's arm. "I don't want you to think I'd do that to you. I'd never just walk out of here."

"I hope not."

"You mean too much to me," Christina said. "Besides, before I accepted this job, Dad had a talk with me. He said I couldn't just think about myself this time. I had to consider the fact that we're sisters, and anything I do might reflect on you."

"Dad said that?"

Christina nodded. "And that's not all he said. It'll take me hours to tell you everything I had to go through with him before I agreed to work here."

"I want you to be yourself. If you ever feel like this isn't the place for you, please let me know."

Christina shrugged then nodded. "I can see where he's coming from. After all, I don't have the best employment history. And I have to admit I hesitated at first. Then I decided to do whatever it took to stick it out, no matter how much I hate the job."

"You hate it?"

"Not yet." Christina smiled and playfully shoved Mandy. "Just kidding. No, I actually like it here, even though standing at the counter is boring."

"All jobs have something not to like," Mandy said. "It's up to you to turn that around. I don't like standing here without something to do, either, which is why I use my time to call people."

"That makes sense." Christina glanced over at the stack of cards that had recently come in. "Do you have a script?"

"Not a script, but the guidelines should be in your training manual." Mandy reached for the manual that Christina had stuck beneath the counter, and she flipped through, until she found the section on follow-up. "Here it is. Read this a couple of times, then we can practice before you place your first call."

"Is that your job?" Christina asked. "I mean, you're the photography trainer, not the phone call trainer."

"I think it's okay for me to do this for you. Our goal isn't to stay in some narrow job description. We want to provide the best service and product to keep our customers happy."

❧

Tony heard every single word between the sisters, even behind the closed office door. He grinned as Mandy helped Christina work through her concerns.

From the moment he saw them interact, he could see the love between them, but he also saw that there were issues, too. Christina had quite a bit to learn about business, but Mandy needed to learn to delegate and not try to do everything herself. *She'd make an awesome mom.* He quickly dropped that thought and forced himself to concentrate on work.

He got up to take over from Mandy. As he opened his office door, both women were standing close, looking at the training manual. His pulse quickened when Mandy turned around and smiled at him.

"I was just showing her some stuff to do when it's slow," Mandy said.

"Good idea."

Christina picked up a card and turned to Mandy. "How about we start now?" She looked at the name on the card. "You can be Mrs. Fielding."

Tony lifted an eyebrow as he looked at Mandy. "We get to see if acting runs in the family."

Mandy rolled her eyes as she laughed. "I'm afraid my sister got all the acting genes."

He hung around and listened as they rehearsed the first time. Christina was actually pretty good at answering the objections Mandy tossed at her.

"You can do this," Mandy said. "Would you be more comfortable with me here, or would you like for us to leave you alone for your first call?"

Christina chewed her lip for a few seconds. "I'm sort of

embarrassed to make a fool of myself in front of you, but if I need help, it'll be nice to know you're right here."

Tony made a quick decision. "I'll go check some bulbs in the studio. Let me know if you need me."

He hovered close to the door during the first part of Christina's call. She stumbled at first, but within seconds, she found her footing. The second call she made came across much more confident.

After he turned on all the lights to make sure the bulbs worked, he joined the women at the counter. "So how's it going?"

Mandy lifted her hands. "My sister is a natural at this!"

"I never doubted that a minute," Tony said.

Christina did a pretend curtsy, flashed a wide smile, and nodded. "I'd like to thank all the little people who believed in me."

Mandy rolled her eyes. "Looks like we've created a monster."

Tony laughed. "I've always liked monsters."

"Such a guy thing to say," Christina said.

"If it quacks like a duck. . ." Tony wiggled his eyebrows. "Okay, you two. Now that you're an expert on follow-up calls, Christina, I need to see Mandy in my office for a few minutes." He turned to Mandy and winked.

"You two run along. I'll be fine," Christina said as she laughed and waved them off. "I'll book as many appointments as I can."

Once he had Mandy behind a closed door, Tony had a chance to observe her without any distractions. She exuded confidence in a quiet sort of way, and she made him feel all was right in the world.

"You needed me?" she asked.

Her choice of words struck him hard. There was no doubt in his mind that God had placed Mandy in his life for a reason, and Tony suspected it wasn't just to have someone nice and trustworthy to work with.

"I talked to Ricco early this morning, and he wants you to

clear your schedule the week after next. We're going ahead with your promotion immediately, so you'll get paid for training."

When she opened her mouth, he thought she might argue with him, but she quickly closed it and smiled. His heart pounded, and warmth filled his soul.

"I appreciate how you've shown your sister some phone techniques, since it's vital to company growth. While she gets comfortable with that, I'd like for you to work with a couple of new part-timers I just hired."

"When do they start?" she asked.

"The day after tomorrow."

Christina tapped her fingernails on the counter. "Are they management trainees, too?"

"No, they're part-time photographers. You can work with them together, and once they catch on, you can spend some time behind the camera with Christina."

❧

After Tony left them alone, Mandy started to say something, but the phone rang. She instinctively reached for it, but Christina beat her to it.

"Small World Portrait Studio, this is Christina, how may I help you?"

Mandy was impressed. Her sister had the spiel down pat, and she had a friendly lilt to her voice.

"Please hold," she said. She punched the HOLD button. "How do I let Tony know he has a call?"

Mandy showed her how to buzz Tony to let him know which line to pick up. Once that was done, she complimented Christina on her phone skills.

"I said what was in the manual. It's easy." Something caught her attention, and she diverted her gaze to something behind Mandy, smiled, and waved.

Mandy turned around and saw Brent from the electronics store. "Be careful with that guy, or you'll never get rid of him."

"Why would I want to get rid of him? I already told you I think he's cute."

"Remember, he's a little nerdy."

Christina giggled. "Nerds are cool. I like the smart guys."

Mandy wasn't so sure how smart Brent was, but if Christina liked him, what did it matter? "So have you had a chance to talk to him?"

"Yes, and we have a date for tomorrow night."

That was a shock. "Why didn't you tell me?"

Christina groaned. "You're acting just like Mom and Dad. I'm a grown woman. I shouldn't have to tell you about everyone I go out with."

"True."

The next appointment came in, so Mandy left Christina in Tony's care. By the time she finished, it was almost time to close up shop.

Brent stood by the door waiting for Christina. Tony saw that, so he offered to walk Mandy to her car.

"Are you okay?" he asked.

She nodded. "Yeah, why?"

He gestured toward Christina and Brent who stood about a foot apart facing each other, with Christina leaning against their mother's car, looking like a flirty teenager. "When Brent showed up, you started acting different."

"I'm just disappointed she didn't tell me about Brent."

"You're not jealous, are you?" he teased.

"No, of course not!"

"Whoa, don't get all worked up. I was just asking."

"Sorry. I guess I was being overly protective of my little sister."

Tony made a humorous face. "I don't think you have to worry about Brent. He seems pretty harmless."

"I'm sure he is."

He backed away from her car. "See you tomorrow, Mandy."

As she pulled away, she thought about how everything in her world changed and how the Lord had such a sure hand in her life.

She rounded the last corner to her house, when her cell phone rang. It was Tony.

"I forgot to ask you something. What are you doing for dinner tonight?" he asked.

"Um. . ." She racked her brain and couldn't think of anything. "I don't know, why?"

"Would you like to go out to dinner with me?"

fifteen

"Um. . ." Mandy thought about the alternative—a microwaved frozen dinner. "Sure, that sounds good."

"Can you be ready in an hour?"

"Absolutely."

As soon as they hung up, Mandy headed straight for her closet. She wanted to look nice but not like she'd put too much effort into it. After skimming her closet for about five minutes, she chose a knee-length pencil skirt and a teal silk blouse Christina had talked her into buying—nothing elaborate, but nice enough to go anywhere.

Tony arrived on the dot, looking more handsome than ever. Even though she'd been with him outside of work before, this felt different—more like a date. That realization alone made her tummy flutter.

"Very pretty," he said. "I like that color on you."

"Thank you." She felt the heat rise to her cheeks. "You look nice, too."

He laughed. "I do clean up well—or so I've heard."

To her surprise, they drove straight to Figaretti's, one of her favorite restaurants in town. The cozy atmosphere added to the intensity of how she was starting to feel toward Tony.

After they ordered, Tony leaned toward her. "I wanted to discuss some things. . . ."

Her heart hammered in her chest, but he'd quit talking. Instead, he studied her face like he'd never seen it before. "What do you want to discuss?"

"I want to talk about—" He glanced away and pursed his lips before turning back to her. "I thought we'd talk about Small World, but I thought it would be better to talk away from the studio."

133

Mandy's heart sank. So this *was* a business dinner. She had to look away to cover her disappointment.

"I've been talking with my uncle about a strategy for the future, and he agrees that we need to work on building more business skills in our managers and encouraging them to hire more part-time photographers. That will take care of two issues—burnout and being able to see who has a knack for the job."

She tried to focus on his words, but her ears rang with embarrassment over her misperception of his intentions. "That makes sense."

He continued. "I'm thinking that I'll probably put Christina in an assistant manager position until I'm sure she's ready to run the studio as a full manager."

"The one here?" Mandy asked. She'd assumed Christina would get her own studio but somewhere else.

"Yes. I think she likes it here, and there's no point in moving her into a situation she's not comfortable with."

"So," Mandy said slowly. "Where will you go?"

He shrugged. "Wherever they need me. After I agreed to work for the family business, they made it very clear that I'd most likely have to move around a bit and travel a great deal more before they settle me in a long-term position."

"Oh." Mandy hated the feelings that bubbled inside her.

"Did I say something wrong?"

She dared a look into his eyes but instantly regretted it. "No." Her throat constricted, causing the word to come out in a squeak.

"Your new position is still on the drawing board. We're trying to decide how we want to use you. Ricco was thinking that we'd bring the full-time photographers here for training, and they could go back to their studios and work with the part-timers."

Mandy nodded. "That makes sense." She felt like she was going through the motions, while all she wanted to do was jump up and run away from Tony.

"It does, but I like my idea better."

At least he was giving her cues to keep her in the conversation. "What's your idea?"

"Since you'll be a regional trainer, you can go to each studio and work with the photographers as a group. That way, the instruction will be consistent." He paused and smiled before adding, "That is, if you don't mind traveling."

"I don't mind. I figured I'd have to travel some."

"Good. You and I are on the same page, then. Fortunately, Ricco is open to our suggestions. It's important to him and my uncle that our management team is happy. That's the only way we'll keep skilled and committed people with the company."

At least her career seemed to be going well. Mandy took a couple of deep breaths and forced a smile. "I'm happy with Small World, and I'm grateful for your confidence."

"But?" He tilted his head and studied her.

"No buts. Everything is going even better than I ever imagined."

"I'm glad."

Their food arrived, so Mandy was able to divert her attention away from Tony's warm brown eyes that melted her insides. He bowed his head, and she followed. He softly said a blessing before they started eating.

They made small talk for a few minutes, until he asked about her mother. "Christina says she's doing well. Have you had a chance to see her?"

Mandy nodded. "She's been busy lately, between all her long walks and the fact that Dad has suddenly turned all his attention toward her. I think it scared him to think he might lose her."

"I can see how that would happen. Sometimes it takes fear to make us realize the importance of something we have."

The way he said that gave Mandy the impression he understood firsthand. "She's lost a few pounds, and Christina said Mom fusses at her when she brings junk food into the house."

"That's understandable."

"Mom used to bake cookies, pies, and cakes all the time. We had dessert after every meal. Now Mom keeps a big bowl filled with fresh fruit."

Tony laughed. "I'm afraid there would have been a mutiny in our house if my mom did that."

"There probably would have been when we were younger, but after our scare and finding out how high her cholesterol was, we're happy she's making these changes."

"I'm glad to hear your mother's doing better. She's been on my family's prayer list."

"Thanks, Tony." Mandy took a sip of her tea as she thought about how nice Tony was. He couldn't help it if she'd developed a crush on him.

When she put her napkin on the table beside her plate, he gestured for the server to bring the check. "I had a wonderful time, Mandy. I think it's a good idea for us to get to know each other better, since we're working on the same team. I think the timing on company growth is perfect, and with you on board, there's no doubt we'll have the best children's photographers in the industry."

Tony had just given her one more reason she couldn't let him know how she felt. His focus was on company growth, nothing else. But when he looked at her again with such a tender expression, she couldn't help the sensation of swirling into an abyss.

The following Sunday, Mandy arrived at church early, so she sat toward the front and saved Christina a spot. When she turned around to watch for her sister, Mandy spotted Tony, who made eye contact right away. He waved then walked toward her as though on a mission. She scooted over more to make more room for him.

"Mind if I join you?" he asked.

"Of course not."

She kept glancing around, looking for Christina, while

Tony chatted with the man next to him. Finally, her sister arrived, arm in arm with Brent.

"I cannot believe what I'm seeing," Mandy said.

Tony turned around and waved. Brent's deer-in-the-headlights expression changed to one of relief. He and Christina made a beeline toward their pew.

Everyone scooted to make room. It was a tight squeeze, so Tony lifted his arm and rested it on the pew behind Mandy. She wanted to snuggle into him, but that obviously wasn't suitable for two very strong reasons—this was church, and he was her boss. Her face flushed.

With so many people in the pew, Mandy and Tony had to share a hymnal for the traditional songs, and they put their heads together to see the contemporary lyrics on the screen in the front of the church. As the tall man on the front row swayed to the music, Tony and Mandy had to move in the opposite direction. After a few times, it became comical, and Mandy let out a giggle. Tony winked and smiled down at her.

After church, Tony walked out to the parking lot with Mandy. "What are you doing this afternoon?" he asked.

"I'm stopping by Mom and Dad's house. They've been so busy, it's hard to catch them home."

Tony grinned. "I'm happy your mother is doing so well."

"I know. We used to think she was content cooking all day, but after her heart attack, she said it was time to really live while she was able to."

"Well, I was going to ask if you wanted to do something."

Mandy wondered if she should risk asking if he'd like to join her. She hesitated for a few seconds before deciding to just go for it.

"Would you like to join me?" she asked. The minute she said that, she second-guessed herself and wanted to take back the invitation. "I mean, my parents really appreciated how much you helped when Mom was in the hospital and all. . . ." She felt like crawling into a hole.

"I'd love to, if you don't think they'd mind."

Mandy's heart raced. "They wouldn't mind in the least."

He nodded. "I miss my family, and the opportunity to spend some time with yours would be nice."

"They used to always have a big spread of food on Sundays, but I'm not sure now."

"I don't want to impose on them at mealtime."

"Trust me, Tony, if there's food, there will be plenty for you and leftovers for a week."

"If you're sure. . ."

"I'm positive. Why don't you come to my apartment in about an hour?" she said. "I can drive us to my parents' house."

"Sounds good."

As soon as Mandy walked into her apartment, she called her parents. Her dad answered. "I wanted to make sure we were still on for this afternoon," she said. "And if you don't mind, I'd like to bring Tony."

"Absolutely." His voice sounded more cheerful than she remembered since she was a little girl. "We went to the early service this morning so we could come home and start cooking."

"You said 'we.' Does this mean you cooked, too?"

"Yep. Your mother told me she doesn't think it's fair that she has all the fun. Just wait until you taste my fruit salad. In your mother's words, it's heavenly."

Mandy laughed. "Can't wait. I'm glad you and Mom are enjoying yourselves."

"After the scare, both of us realized we'd been on a treadmill, doing things we'd always done, and not truly enjoying God's blessings."

After they hung up, Mandy rocked back on her heels and thought about what her dad had said. She'd never thought of her parents as unhappy, but they didn't exactly exude joy, either. Now they sparkled with laughter and happiness every time she saw them. Her mom even said that her heart attack was the best thing that could have happened to their marriage.

The more Mandy thought about her parents, the more

she pondered her own life. Basically, she was guilty of doing exactly what her parents had always done in the past—running on a treadmill and hoping nothing bad would happen. She'd wanted to be promoted to manager of the studio, but other than that, she never put much thought into anything else she might want.

Now that she had the surprise promotion to photography trainer, Mandy decided it was time to take stock of what she had, decide what she really wanted in life, and make plans based on what was in her control. She couldn't do any of that without His help, so she bowed her head and prayed for guidance, wisdom, and the ability to recognize opportunity— both professional and personal.

❧

The first thing Tony noticed when Mandy opened her door was a sense of self-awareness he hadn't seen before. She smiled and invited him in.

"Mom and Dad know you're coming. I hope you're hungry."

He lifted his eyebrows. "I didn't mean to invite myself for lunch, but I never turn down good food."

Her smile was warm but filled with amusement. "This will be good, as in healthy for you. I have no idea how it'll taste without Mom's trademark butter, salt, and sugar."

Tony patted his belly. "I could stand to eat a healthy meal, so I won't complain." He gestured toward the door. "Ready?"

"Yeah, let's go."

"Mind if I drive?" he asked.

She shrugged. "It doesn't matter to me."

He pointed his remote toward his car to unlock it. "Good. I have to admit I'm a little nervous, and driving will give me something to do with my hands."

Her eyes twinkled as she smiled at him. "That's cute."

On the way to her parents' house, Tony asked questions about her upbringing. "Christina doesn't seem like the domestic type. How about you?"

"Neither of us has a domestic bone in our bodies. Mom

took care of everything, from food to cleaning. We just had to maintain our rooms and help out with one chore a day."

As they came to a light, he contorted his mouth and cut his gaze to her. "I hate to admit this, but until I went into the army, I didn't even do that. All I had to do was make my bed every morning."

"So you were spoiled, huh?"

He shrugged. "I don't know if you could call me spoiled. I always appreciated everything, and I found ways to make my spending money. My parents didn't believe in unearned allowance."

"Same here. We didn't get a dime until Mom checked our chore list to make sure everything was done." She sighed. "I just wish I'd learned how to cook."

"It's never too late to learn."

"True. My dad's proof of that."

She turned her head to look out the window, giving him a nice view of her profile. Mandy was very pretty, but what he liked most about her profile was the way her chin jutted when she was deep in thought.

Before the light turned green, she turned and looked him directly in the eye. Everything around him seemed to swirl out of focus—everything but Mandy. At that moment, he knew he was falling in love.

She pointed to the light. "You can go now."

"Oh, yeah." His voice came out scratchy. "I was distracted."

Out of the corner of his eye, he noticed her every movement. He wanted to reach over and take one of her hands in his, but he didn't dare do it—not until he had some idea how she felt about him. The last thing he needed was to make their situation awkward as long as they had to work together.

As they walked up the sidewalk to the Pruitts' house, Christina flung open the door. Brent was right behind her, grinning.

"Hey, you two," Brent said. "Don't tell me you're an item now."

Tony felt like someone had stolen the air out of his lungs.

He stopped in his tracks and waited to see Mandy's reaction. To his dismay, she let out a nervous giggle but didn't say a word. Instead, she walked right past Christina and Brent.

Not knowing what else to do, Tony followed her through the house, to the kitchen, where her parents stood on either side of an island. Her dad was peeling fruit, and her mother was garnishing a vegetable platter.

"We're just about ready to eat," her mother said as she pointed to the counter behind her. "Why don't you each grab one of those bowls over there and carry them into the dining room?"

Mr. Pruitt chuckled. "This is the first time Mandy's young man has been to the house, and you're putting him to work already?"

❧

Mandy wanted to crawl into a hole and never come out. Her young man? How could her dad do that to her?

Tony reached for a bowl. "I don't mind."

Avoiding his gaze, Mandy grabbed a bowl and led the way to the dining room. Once they were alone, she turned to him. "Sorry about that, Tony. I don't think my dad meant anything by that."

"Too bad." He set the bowl down on the table and closed the distance between them. The only thing in their way was the bowl in her hands. "I was kind of hoping he knew something I didn't know."

"Huh?" She tilted her head as she waited for him to explain.

For the first time since she'd met Tony, he looked ill at ease. After shuffling his feet and looking around the room for a couple of seconds, he blurted, "Mandy, my feelings for you are growing. I'm sorry if this makes you uncomfortable, but no matter how hard I try to keep our relationship strictly professional, I feel myself falling in love with you."

sixteen

Mandy stood there and stared at Tony, not believing what she just heard. Here he was, one of the best-looking guys she'd ever seen in her life, his future mapped out by the good fortune of being born into a family with a growing business, exuding kindness like she'd never seen before. Why would he be interested in her?

"Um. . ." She nervously glanced over her shoulder to see if anyone else was behind her. When she turned back around to face Tony, she didn't know what to say.

He shoved his hands into his pockets and looked down at his feet. "Well, I guess I just got my answer."

"Your answer?"

Emotion sparked in his eyes as he met her gaze. "You don't feel it, do you?"

"I—I just don't know what to say."

He let out a small snicker of resignation. "You don't have to say anything, Mandy. I just took a big risk that didn't pay off."

Mandy set the bowl on the table and turned back to face Tony. She was about to let him know that she felt the same way when her sister and Brent burst into the room.

"Hey there!" Brent made a snorting sound. "So they put you to work, huh?"

Mandy's heart sank. She couldn't very well discuss her feelings with Tony with other people around.

Tony nodded and motioned for everyone to follow him. "Let's see what else we can do to help."

After all the food was on the table, everyone bowed their heads. Mandy's dad said the blessing. When she lifted her head afterward, she thought about how cozy they were—her whole family here, and everyone part of a couple.

"Mom, this looks and tastes wonderful," Christina said after she ate a couple of bites. "I didn't know healthy food could be this good."

"I know," their mother replied. "When the doctor first told me I needed to change my lifestyle, I wondered if it was worth living for." When everyone groaned, she gestured for them to quiet down. "But once I found some fun activities and your father brought me some new cookbooks, I see how much better life can be."

"I need to start eating like this," Tony said. "Maybe you can share some recipes."

Mom smiled and tilted her head as she looked at Tony. "You cook?"

"Not much, but I think I should probably start."

"I didn't cook before," Dad said. "But now I like to putter around in the kitchen, and it's kind of fun."

If someone had told Mandy about this conversation a year earlier, she never would have believed it. In fact, this whole scenario seemed unreal—with her sister coming back from Hollywood and fawning over geeky Brent, her boss Tony having dinner with her family after admitting he had romantic feelings for her, and her parents eating fresh, natural food that they cooked together.

Christina clearly hung on every word Brent said, which obviously pleased him to no end. Mandy studied them with interest. When she turned to Tony, she saw that he'd been observing her.

"Want some applesauce cake?" her mother asked after everyone put down their forks. "It's low cal, low fat, and delicious."

"I'm stuffed," Mandy said. "But I'll be glad to take some home for later."

Everyone pitched in to clear the table. Tony volunteered to do the dishes, so Mandy could spend some time with her family. Brent took a hint and joined him in the kitchen.

"Your young men are certainly thoughtful," their dad said

as they settled in the family room.

Christina beamed. "Brent is the sweetest, most wonderful man I've ever met."

"He certainly seems to be into you, too," Mandy said.

"Just like Tony is into you." Christina grinned. "Looks like we both found love at the same time."

Before Tony's admission before dinner, Mandy would have argued that point, but now she wasn't sure what to say. She didn't want to discuss it with Christina yet.

Mandy decided to change the subject. "Mom, dinner was wonderful."

"Who knew healthy food could be so delicious?" Her mother beamed. "And you'll be happy to know that your father and I have joined the Hundred-Mile Club."

"Hundred-Mile Club?" Christina grimaced. "That's a lot of miles. Are you sure you can do that?"

"Of course we can. We just had to sign a statement that we walked, ran, biked, or swam a hundred miles per quarter. It's through our senior group. As long as we do that every three months, we can stay in."

"Cool. Maybe I should do that," Christina said.

"Sorry, sweetie." Their mother gave her an apologetic look. "You have to be over fifty-five."

Christina frowned. "That's discrimination."

The rest of the family laughed. Tony and Brent appeared at the door.

"We've been thinking about a way to start a fitness program for Small World," Tony said. "It's been a challenge since we're spread out all over the country. Maybe we can start something similar."

Christina's eyes lit up. "I'll be the first to join." She turned to Mandy. "You'll do it, too, right?"

Mandy shrugged. "If you can do it, I'm sure I can."

"What's that supposed to mean?"

"Girls!" Their dad lifted a finger. "I'm sure your sister didn't mean anything by her comment, Christina. And, Mandy, be more careful about how you word things, okay?"

Mandy looked over at Tony, who was obviously trying to hide a grin. "Okay, Dad."

"All the dishes are done," Tony said. "Anything else you need while we're here?"

Mandy's mom got up. "You boys are very sweet. Our daughters sure know how to pick 'em."

Christina beamed at Brent, while Mandy felt her cheeks flame. She stood and walked over to the door. "We really need to go. Thanks for everything, Mom and Dad. Dinner was delicious."

"Don't forget your applesauce cake. I'll get some plastic containers so y'all can take some home."

Mandy and Tony waited for their cake then left. As soon as they pulled up to the stop sign at the end of the street, Tony glanced at Mandy. "Your family reminds me of my own. Very loving and fun."

"And centered on food?"

He laughed. "Yeah, that, too."

"Sometimes God lets things happen to get our attention."

Tony slowed down for the stop sign, looked to see that there were no cars coming, and turned to Mandy. "Yes, I know—things we never expected." He reached for her hand and lifted it to his lips for a light kiss.

Mandy gasped. She wanted to say something, but her brain wouldn't cooperate. Her breath caught in her throat.

After Tony accelerated past the stop sign, Mandy studied his profile as she thought about what he'd said earlier. "Mandy?" He let go of her hand, sending disappointment surging through her. "I hope my admission of my feelings didn't make you too uncomfortable."

She cleared her throat. "You surprised me."

"I know, and I'm sorry."

"Oh, don't be sorry. Please. I sort of, well. . ." Mandy had never told a guy she loved him. The very thought of doing so made her palms sweat.

"You don't have to say anything. I understand."

"No, I want to say something. It's just that I've never been like this before."

"Been like what?" he said, cutting his gaze over to her for a split second before turning his attention back to the road.

She sucked in a breath before blurting, "I've never been in love before."

Tony immediately pulled into a business center parking lot and parked before completely turning around to face her.

"Are you now?"

Her ears rang, and her heart pounded as she nodded. "Yes, I'm pretty sure I am."

He leaned back. "With me?"

She nodded.

"This is great news!" He reached for her hand again and dropped a kiss on the back of it.

"I hope it's okay, though," she said. "I mean, I love my job at Small World, and I don't want to do anything that isn't—"

"It's fine, Mandy. We obviously don't have a problem with family members working together. This is different. I'll talk to Ricco and Uncle Ed about it, but I'm sure they'll be happy."

"What if they're not?"

"I'll be surprised, but we'll deal with it then. Right now, I just want to enjoy knowing you feel the same way I do."

She opened her mouth to thank him, but that seemed awkward, so she clamped it shut. Even during her last relationship, she knew the guy wasn't *the one*. She liked him quite a bit, but she never felt that she was in love like she was now.

He pulled up in front of her apartment and got out to walk her to her door. "You weren't kidding about there being plenty of food. I haven't eaten this much since the last time I went to a family reunion. My mother and her sisters like to outdo each other." He patted his belly. "At least after today, I don't have to worry about all the cholesterol."

"Would you like to come in?" she asked.

Tony hesitated then shook his head. "Maybe some other time. I need to get back to my place and clean up a bit then call my mother." He took a couple of steps back. "See you tomorrow, Mandy."

&

Tony had been tempted to abandon everything just so he could spend more time with Mandy, but it was time to call his mother. He hadn't missed a Sunday afternoon yet. One thing he knew was that he needed to clean his apartment before the call because the first question out of his mother's mouth was if he was living in a pigsty. It was funny, but he also knew she was serious. His mother had always been a neatnik. Her motto was: "A cluttered house means a cluttered mind, and you can't get anything done in either."

Since he hadn't been home much, it didn't take long to straighten up, dust, and vacuum. Before he punched in his mother's phone number, he prayed that he'd be able to say the right things that would ease her mind. After his last move back to Atlanta, she'd begged him to stay. When his uncle asked him to work in West Virginia, she'd been upset, until he assured her Tony'd likely be back in a year or two.

He expected that she'd be waiting by the phone, so he was surprised when she didn't pick it up until after the third ring. "What took you so long?" he asked.

"You think I wait by the phone every Sunday?"

"Um—yes." He laughed.

She clicked her tongue. "Maybe I do sometimes, but today, I'm busy. I had a bunch of people over for Sunday dinner. I heard some good news from Ed and Ricco."

"You did? Wanna share?" He expected to hear something about their opinion of Mandy, since she'd made such a good impression during her trip to the home office.

"I don't know if I'm supposed to tell you this, but they didn't say not to, so I might as well." She paused for a few seconds to catch her breath before blurting, "You're coming home soon!"

"I'm what?"

"You heard me. Ricco said he thinks you'll have someone to take over the studio in West Virginia, and he needs you in the home office."

"But. . ." Several months ago, before he had a chance to develop feelings for Mandy, Tony would have been elated. But now, West Virginia was beginning to feel like home to him.

"I'll be so happy to have you back home where you belong."

Tony didn't want to upset his mother, but he also needed to let her know how he felt. "Mom, I really like it here."

He expected an argument or at least one of her signature gasps. Instead, he got a giggle. "It's that girl, isn't it?"

"What girl?" So Ricco or Ed *had* mentioned Mandy.

"You know exactly what girl I'm talking about. I hear she's very pretty."

"She is, Mom. Very pretty. But more important than that, she loves the Lord."

"I wouldn't expect otherwise, Tony. You have a good head on your shoulders."

"I had dinner with her family today. They remind me a lot of our family."

He could practically hear his mother smiling through the phone. "So tell me all about them."

Over the next five minutes, Tony talked nonstop about Mandy's family, the food, and how her parents drew closer in the kitchen after her mother's heart attack.

"They sound very sweet." She sniffled. "I wish your father was still alive. I think he would have enjoyed something like that."

Tony knew that once his mother got on the subject of his dad, she was likely to wind up in a full sob. Sometimes that was fine because she needed the release, but he wanted her to be happy now.

"Mom, is there any way you can come up here for a visit soon?"

"Now that you're inviting me, yes. Ed said I could come

with him and Cissy next week—that is, if it's not too soon."

Tony laughed. "I'm fine with that. I'd love to have you."

"So is your apartment a pigsty?"

"I'm keeping it clean. Not as clean as you would, but I think you'll be pleased."

"As long as you don't leave your underwear on the floor and dishes in the sink overnight." She paused before adding, "You don't, do you?"

"No, Mom, I'm good about picking up after myself."

"So tell me more about your girlfriend."

"Haven't I told you enough?"

"You told me about having lunch with her family, but I want to know more about her. You said she loves the Lord. You've been to church with her, right? What is her church like?"

"It reminds me a lot of the church I went to when I was in Atlanta."

"The one you took me to?"

"Yes," he replied.

"Good. How about her cooking skills? Is she a decent cook?"

"I really don't know, but that doesn't really matter to me."

"Ya know, I couldn't cook when I first married your father." He'd heard this story many times. "Yes, Mom, I know."

"But he married me with the understanding that I'd learn from his mother because my mother was German, and she couldn't cook the kind of food he liked."

"So what are you saying?" he teased.

"I'm not saying anything you can't figure out for yourself. Just make sure she's willing to bend a little before you get too serious."

"Don't rush this thing. I just told her how I felt this afternoon."

"Your father and I got engaged three months after we met. How long have you known this girl?"

"Four months."

"How much do you see her?"

"Almost every day." He smiled as he pictured his mother calculating the amount of time they spent together.

"And you're with her all day at work. That's long enough."

"Long enough for what?"

"This mother didn't raise a fool, Tony. You know exactly what I'm talking about."

seventeen

Tony had to hand it to his mother—she didn't hold back. After he got off the phone, he sat and stared at the wall, thinking of what to do next. Even though Small World didn't have a policy against their employees marrying, there was the matter of logistics. He couldn't very well ask Mandy to give up the career she clearly wanted just to make him happy, and their positions were likely to take them to very different places.

Finally, after pondering it as long as he could without obsessing, he got up and headed to the kitchen. He'd kept his place neat, but since his mother was coming, it had to be better than that. He opened the refrigerator and started tossing stuff he knew he'd never finish—mostly leftovers from restaurants.

❧

Mandy went to work the next morning with some trepidation. Now that she and Tony had opened up and said they loved each other, she worried that work might be awkward.

As soon as she opened the door, her sister looked up from her notebook and greeted her with a smile. "I love this job!" Christina exclaimed.

Mandy grinned. "What brought that on?"

"Tony told me I'm doing really well, and he wants me to move on a fast track."

"Wow, Christina, that's wonderful." Mandy walked past her toward the spare office to put her purse down. She passed by Tony's office and heard him talking on the phone. When she came back out, her sister was still busy reading the notebook. "When did he tell you this?"

"First thing this morning. He was here when I got in. . ." She glanced at her watch before looking back at Mandy.

"About half an hour ago."

"Why so early?"

Christina's cheeks flushed. "Brent offered me a ride to work, and since he had to get in early, I figured I could get ahead on my studying."

Mandy had never seen her sister so happy about a man or a job. She'd had more than her fair share of guys stumbling all over themselves when she was younger.

"You really like Brent, don't you?" Mandy asked.

Christina nodded. "He's the sweetest, smartest, and most caring guy I've ever dated." She shrugged and added, "It doesn't hurt that he's cute, too."

Cuteness, like beauty, was definitely in the eye of the beholder, Mandy thought. Tony was cute. Brent was—well, simply okay.

"Would you mind handing me the appointment book? I know we have several scheduled sessions today, but I don't know the specific times."

Christina pulled out the book and passed it to Mandy. "Tony wants me to observe at least one of the sessions."

"That's fine." Mandy caught sight of Tony out of the corner of her eye as he appeared at the door. "Hi." Suddenly, she felt awkward and didn't know what to do with her hands.

He smiled. "So do you mind working with Christina on the cameras a bit today?"

"I'll be glad to." Mandy cleared her throat. "I can show her some camera basics between appointments, too."

"Perfect." He glanced at Christina. "You can practice taking pictures of Mandy."

"No." The word came out automatically. "I mean, I'm sure we can find something else to photograph—maybe a stuffed animal grouping."

Tony folded his arms, tilted his head, and looked at her with curiosity. "That's nothing like having a real, live subject. Especially a reluctant subject. You know that, Mandy."

"Yeah, but—"

Christina spoke up. "My sister has never liked having her picture taken. She's been like that all her life."

Tony's lips quirked into a smile. "I can't imagine why, as pretty as she is."

"I know," Christina said as she turned back to face Mandy, who wanted to crawl into a hole from way too much attention.

"Okay, whatever," Mandy said. "But now I need to get the props in place for the first appointment."

Tony walked around behind the counter. "Why don't you help her, Christina? You need to know every aspect of how to run this place, since I hope to have you in charge soon."

On their way to the back part of the studio, Christina let out a faint squeal. "I have to pinch myself. I can't believe how perfect this job is for me."

Mandy nodded. "You do catch on quickly."

Christina frowned as she stopped, grabbed Mandy's arm, and turned her around. "You didn't think I could do this, did you?"

"I had no doubt you could do it," Mandy said as she tried to think of the right words that wouldn't upset her sister. "The only concern I had was how committed you were to the job. Your whole life, all you talked about was how much you wanted to be famous." She held her breath until Christina smiled, then she let it out.

"I think most girls want to be famous at some time or other. After I got to Hollywood, I saw that it wasn't everything I thought it was. It's a lot of hard work, and there's always someone who wants to drag you down."

"I can imagine," Mandy said.

Christina shook her head. "Not to mention the faith issue. I can't even begin to tell you how difficult it is to hold on to Jesus in the midst of all those distractions."

Mandy thought her heart would burst, she was so proud of her sister. "You were smart to come back." She took a couple of steps toward the cameras then stopped again and turned back to Christina. "I have complete confidence in you, now that you've grown up and taken charge of your life."

Tears formed in Christina's eyes as she pulled her lips between her teeth. Mandy hugged her then gave her a gentle push toward the cameras.

"It's time to learn the parts of the camera and how they work."

"I'm ready." Christina rubbed her hands together. "So show me your stuff."

They spent the next half hour going over the different aspects of the camera—all things Christina needed to know before taking pictures. When the first appointment arrived, she stood beside Mandy and helped with the props. Mandy was delighted by how well her sister related to the children.

Mandy showed Christina the card she kept with notes about the family. She pointed to the comment, "Treats allowed." Christina nodded and picked up the basket filled with candy.

After they had all the pictures organized on the computer, Mandy let Christina help the family choose the shots they wanted. At first, she disagreed with the parents, saying their choices weren't the best, but Mandy pulled her aside and explained that the ultimate choice wasn't hers. The parents were delighted with the pictures. They left smiling.

"Now let's go back and practice," Mandy said. "If I'd known I was having my picture taken today, I would have worn more makeup."

Christina made a face and waved off her comment. "You've always been gorgeous without a speck of makeup. I'm the one who had to cake it on."

"You're kidding, right?" Mandy laughed. "You were always the pretty one, and I was the smart one."

"Well, I just happen to think we're both pretty and smart. I think a better way of putting it would be: I'm the confident one, and you're the one who needs a better self-image."

Mandy couldn't argue with her there. "Whatever."

"So show me what to do again," Christina said as she inspected the camera. "I turn this little thingy, then I press this?"

She might not have grasped the terminology, but she quickly caught on. Over the next half hour, Christina had taken dozens of pictures of Mandy.

By the time they finished putting everything away and got back to the front counter, Tony already had Mandy's pictures up on the computer screen. "Nice," he said in a low, appreciative tone. "Very nice." He grinned at Mandy. "You're an excellent trainer."

Mandy felt her cheeks flame as Christina joined him and started talking about how good she looked. "Look at the skin tone in this one. She looks like a professional model."

"Better," he argued. "I've never seen a professional model with such great proportions."

"Hey, you two," Mandy said from the back of the counter. "I'm right here."

"Come look at this." Christina gestured her over. "If you don't mind my saying so, I'm an excellent photographer."

Mandy took a chance and glanced at the photos. Her eyes widened. "Is that me?"

Christina did a double take before laughing. "Yes, who did you think it was? The Cookie Monster?"

Tony cast a silly look at Mandy. "The Cookie Monster wishes. Seriously, these are some great shots. Mandy, you did a great job of showing Christina how to take good pictures."

As Mandy studied the shots, she realized that Christina really did have a natural eye for photography. Not everyone knew when to snap the picture. Obviously, Christina did. After Tony clicked onto the next page, and the shots got even better, she nodded.

"Good job, sis." She was still embarrassed about being the subject, and she didn't know what else to do, so she rolled her eyes.

Tony backed away from the counter. "I think I'll go to my

office now and let the two of you discuss photography."

As soon as he was out of hearing range, Christina planted her fists on her hips. "What is going on?"

Leaning against the counter, Mandy slowly shook her head from side to side. "Things are so different now. They're happening so fast. I'm not sure how to deal with them. I have no idea what to do."

"Wanna discuss it later?"

&

After seeing the amazing pictures Christina took of Mandy, two important thoughts hit him hard. Christina could wind up being as good a photographer as her sister with the training she was getting, and the photographs had captured the inner beauty he'd seen in Mandy since he first met her. Her eyes sparkled with joy, and the slight tilt of her head showed a playful side that not everyone could see. Her smile could brighten the darkest of rooms.

Tony called his mother to find out what time she was arriving at his apartment on Friday. She said she was coming to the studio first, and she'd go to the apartment with him.

He had a good idea why she wanted to come straight to the studio. "That's fine," he said.

"Don't worry about cleaning for me," she said. "I can do that while I'm there."

"Don't be silly, Mom. I'm a grown man, and I can clean my own apartment."

She laughed. "You might be grown to the rest of the world, but you'll always be my sweet boy, Anthony."

"Ssh. Don't say that again." He lowered his voice. "Someone might hear you."

"Oh, trust me, Tony, I won't tell Mandy that."

"I didn't say anything about Mandy."

"No, but I can't wait to meet her." She paused before asking, "She will be there Friday when I arrive, right?"

His suspicion had been confirmed. "Yes, she'll be here. Uncle Ed is meeting with her, remember?"

"Good." He could practically hear his mother grinning over the phone.

He hung up and went back out to the front desk, where Christina was studying her books. She glanced up and gestured for him.

"Need something?" he asked.

She nodded. "What if someone either doesn't order pictures, or they want to add to their package later? Can they come back and order them later?"

"Yes, we try to get them to place an order, but we don't like to pressure people."

"Okay, good. I'm thinking that someone might start out wanting the special then change their mind and want a bigger package after they see how cute their kids are."

"Happens all the time," he said. "We keep the pictures in the system for at least a year."

A woman stepped out of the studio and approached the desk. "Are you Christina?" she asked.

Christina nodded. "May I help you with something?"

"Mandy wants to see you."

Tony nodded toward the back. "Go see what she wants. I'll watch the desk."

As soon as Christina left, Tony glanced down at the notebook page Christina and saw the copious notes she'd jotted in the margins. He smiled at how thorough she was and how seriously she seemed to be taking this job.

◆

Mandy stepped away from the camera and motioned for the children to be still. Their mother stood to the side, smiling.

"Christina, would you like to give me a hand?"

"Sure, what do you need?"

Mandy waved her hand toward the camera. "You can take their pictures."

Christina's eyebrows shot up. "You mean, like, for real?"

Both Mandy and the children's mother cracked up laughing. "Yes, for real. I've already discussed it with Mrs. Martin, and she's more than happy to let you work with her kids."

"That's right," the woman said. "We're regular customers, so you'll be seeing us again in a few months."

"Oh, okay." Christina tentatively stepped behind the camera and made a couple of adjustments. She was tentative at first, and she asked for Mandy's help.

"You'll do just fine as long as you do what I taught you," Mandy assured her as she took a step back. "If you mess up, we'll just do them over."

Within minutes, Christina had taken several pictures and adjusted the children's positions for more shots.

"She's very good with them," Mrs. Martin whispered. "Where did you find her?"

Mandy grinned at her favorite customer. "She's my sister."

"All done," Christina said. She grabbed the goodie basket and passed out stickers and candy. "Y'all were great! Have two—" She glanced over her shoulder at Mrs. Martin, who nodded before she pulled more candy from the basket.

After Christina finished with the children, they joined their mother and Mandy. Christina was right behind them.

"Your sister, huh?" Mrs. Martin said.

Christina took a couple of steps toward Mandy until they were side by side. "I'm the baby."

Mrs. Martin laughed, tilted her head, and looked back and forth between Mandy and Christina, then slowly nodded. "Yes, as a matter of fact, I can definitely see the resemblance. It's nice that you work together so well."

"She taught me everything I know," Christina said as she put her arm around Mandy and squeezed. "I still have a lot to learn."

"Don't we all?" Mrs. Martin said as she walked toward the reception area. "I'll take the kids to the sandwich shop while you get the pictures ready."

The second the Martin family left, Tony lifted a finger. "I need to talk to both of you before you work on the pictures."

"Okay," Mandy said. "One at a time or together?"

She watched as he made his decision. "Why don't I talk to you first, and Christina can watch the counter. You know how to pull the proofs up, right?"

Christina nodded. "Sure. I'll get them arranged how I think they should be while y'all talk."

Mandy followed Tony into his office. He went around behind his desk and told her to close the door.

"You know my uncle's coming, right?"

She nodded. "Yes. I have everything ready to discuss my new position."

"Good." He leaned back in his chair and took a deep breath. "My mother will be with him."

"Your mother?" Mandy asked. "I didn't know she worked for the company."

"Oh, she doesn't. She just wants to spend time with me and—well, to meet you."

eighteen

Mandy gulped and forced a smile, hoping Tony wouldn't see her distress. "I'm looking forward to meeting her, too."

Tony laughed. "She's not too bad."

"What's that supposed to mean?"

"She doesn't bite." A grin remained on his face as he shook his head. "My mom is one of the sweetest women I've ever met. Very capable, too. In fact, she reminds me of you."

Mandy pursed her lips before retorting, "So you like me because I remind you of your mother?"

"Maybe some." The corners of his lips twitched.

"At least you admit it."

Tony reached out and gently glided his hand across her cheek, sending shivers throughout her body. "You're both Christian women who are capable of doing anything you want to do. However, your goals are completely different from hers."

Mandy folded her arms and tilted her head. "How so?"

"She's always been perfectly happy staying home, baking, and telling us kids what to do. You, on the other hand, are career focused."

"I like what I do," she said. "The kids are great."

With a chuckle, Tony backed away. "Maybe you and my mother are alike on that point, too. She loves children with every fiber of her being."

"Mandy, I need your help!"

The sound of Christina's voice burst the invisible bubble that had formed around Mandy and Tony. "I'll be right there."

As Mandy helped Christina set up for the next photography session, she thought about the conversation with Tony. He'd always been open—even in the beginning when they'd first met—and he let it be known he didn't even want to be in

Wheeling. And as he gradually accepted his position, he admitted how he'd misjudged everything.

As the next few days passed, Christina grew more and more competent with the camera. Mandy and Tony were both impressed.

"Do you really think she'll be ready to manage the studio soon?" Mandy asked.

He rubbed his chin as he thought it over. "She could probably do it now, if we let her."

"I don't know about that."

"You're her sister. At some point, you need to let go and allow her to make some mistakes."

Mandy nodded. "True. I certainly made my share of them."

"You've done a good job of training her."

"Thank you."

Tony licked his lips and stared at her for a moment before doing an about-face. As he walked away, Mandy wondered what he'd been thinking.

❧

Friday morning, Mandy stood at the counter going over the day's schedule. She was about to tell Christina that Tony's aunt, uncle, and mother would be in, but before she had a chance, her sister's eyebrows shot up, and her eyes widened.

Mandy glanced over her shoulder to see what her sister was looking at. Through the glass window, she spotted a couple of women standing on the sidewalk beside a shiny red convertible. One woman was smoothing down her hair, while the other was looking up and down the street as if trying to find something. Edward joined them on the sidewalk. As he guided the women toward the front door, Mandy felt her mouth grow dry and her stomach flutter.

"That's Edward Rossi, his wife, and Tony's mom," Mandy whispered.

"Oh," Christina said, nodding her head. "No wonder your face is bright red."

Mandy groaned. She couldn't play it cool if she tried. She

took a couple of deep breaths, trying to relax before Mr. Rossi opened the door for the others.

The first woman in the door zeroed in on Mandy. "Oh, you must be the girl I've heard so much about."

Mandy heard her sister snickering behind her. She cleared her throat.

"I'm Maria, Tony's mother," the woman said as she approached Mandy with open arms.

"I'm Mandy."

Mr. Rossi and his wife, Cissy, introduced themselves to Christina, who was the epitome of professionalism. She shook their hands and offered them a tour of the studio. As soon as Maria let go of Mandy, the sisters followed the others to the back. Tony joined them.

"You've got good reports, Tony," Mr. Rossi said. "I'm sure it must have something to do with these lovely ladies."

Christina spoke up. "It's probably because of my sister's hard work. She really knows her stuff."

Mandy appreciated Christina's efforts, but she was embarrassed. "It's all of us."

"Where are the part-timers?" Mr. Rossi asked.

"They're not able to work the hours we need, and the last one I hired didn't show up," Tony replied. "That's why I've been looking for more people."

Mr. Rossi nodded. "It's tough to keep a solid staff of part-time help."

Christina cleared her throat, and all heads turned to face her. "I've contacted one of the local senior citizen groups to see if anyone wants to supplement their social security income. Of course I asked my sister first, and she said I could give it a try."

Mr. Rossi rubbed his chin. "What a great idea. They're more likely to stick around than a student, and if they need the money, they'll work the hours you ask them to."

"Plus they don't need to worry about child care, and they won't expect too many hours," Christina added.

Tony tilted his head. "I had no idea you did that, Christina. I agree with Uncle Ed—it's a great idea. Why didn't you say something to me about it?"

"I just called them late yesterday. I was gonna talk to you sometime today, and. . .well, the opportunity just presented itself." She cast a sheepish glance Mandy's way then turned back to Tony. "I hope you're not too upset."

"Oh, I'm not upset in the least," Tony said. "I'm just glad you took the initiative."

"Which brings me to a very important announcement," Mr. Rossi said. "We've decided it's time to bring you back to Atlanta, now that you have capable people to run this place."

Mandy felt like her heart had dropped to the floor, and someone had stomped on it. She pulled her cheeks between her teeth to keep from showing a reaction.

"That is, if my son wants to come back to Atlanta," Maria said softly.

Christina looked at Mandy with concern, but she didn't say a word. Everyone grew quiet, until Mr. Rossi spoke up again.

"Mandy, do you have some time to discuss your new position?"

She nodded. "Yes."

Mr. Rossi asked Maria and Cissy to go shopping for a little while and come back for him later. "Or you can go to the hotel," he added.

"Shopping sounds great to me," Maria said. "Too bad these girls have to work, or they could go with us."

"My sister isn't much of a shopper," Christina blurted. "But I love it."

Maria winked at Mandy. "To be honest, I'm not all that much of a shopper, either. I'd much rather be in the kitchen cooking for my family."

Mr. Rossi patted his belly that hung over his belt. "Cissy doesn't mind cooking, either, but she used to be quite a shopper before we had kids." He quickly resumed his professional stance and gestured toward the office area. "After you, Mandy."

Mandy was about to sit closer to the door, but Mr. Rossi encouraged her to go behind the desk. "I don't want you to be uncomfortable," he said. "Now that you're on the management team, you're like family."

Her lips twitched into a smile. "Thanks."

"So have you thought about some of the things you'd like to do in your trainer position?"

She nodded. "I've made some notes."

"Okay, let's discuss them." He gestured for her to go ahead of him. "By the way, I'd like you to call me Edward or just Ed. This Mr. Rossi thing makes me feel old."

Mandy grinned. "Okay. . .Edward."

Two hours later, they'd finished talking about how she'd do her job. He'd asked if she preferred traveling or having new photographers come to her. She said it didn't matter—that she'd do whatever was needed in each specific case.

"That's good," he said. "It's hard for some people to leave their families. How about you come to Atlanta again? Is your mother healthy enough for you to leave?"

"She's doing great," Mandy said. "I'm proud of how she's changed her lifestyle, so it won't happen again."

"Yeah, Tony told me she's a great cook."

Mandy was dying to hear what else Tony had said, but she didn't want to come right out and ask. Instead, she just smiled.

"Okay," Edward said as he stood. "That about does it. I'll come in tomorrow and on Monday to handle some issues with Tony and get to know Christina a little better, since we're turning this place over to her. The two of you need to start interviewing some more photographers."

"When will we need to do this?"

"Right away. I want to bring Tony back to Atlanta in a month to six weeks."

Mandy looked down to keep him from seeing her expression. When she felt like she could look at him without showing how she felt, she saw the tenderness in his expression.

"We also need to discuss where we place your office, too, Mandy. Since this is such a new thing for us, we're not sure if we want you to remain in a studio or if you should be in the home office. Of course, we wouldn't want you to leave your mother if she needs you."

Mandy licked her lips. "Thank you."

After he left the office, she remained sitting there staring at the blotter on the desk. Before her mother's heart attack, she wouldn't have minded moving for her job, but after the scare with her mother, she felt the tug to stay in West Virginia. Besides, she and Christina had just begun to forge a new, more adult sisterly relationship, and the experience was amazing. After the great news of her promotion, she should have been in a much better mood.

Tony appeared at the door. "Uncle Ed wants to meet with me. He said it won't take long, so you and Christina can go to lunch as soon as we're done."

Mandy took a few minutes to gather her thoughts before she got up and joined her sister at the front. Christina looked up with a broad smile.

"Isn't this the best company ever?" Christina said. "I'll never be able to thank you enough for finding this place."

Mandy forced herself to smile back. "Yes, it's a very good company."

Christina leaned toward her with a look of concern. "What's wrong, Mandy? Did I do something?"

"No, you didn't do a thing."

With a tight jaw, Christina looked around the corner then whispered, "Did Tony say something to upset you?"

"No."

"Okay, I give up. Tell me what's got you all upset."

Mandy was tempted to tell her nothing and pretend everything was fine. But she couldn't. She needed to vent.

"Just when I fell in love with someone who loves the Lord, loves me, and is everything I want in a guy, things go haywire."

"You mean like Tony going back to Atlanta?" Christina asked.

Mandy nodded. "He's never made it a secret about his plan. In fact, when he first got here, he openly resented being made to work at the studio level. He wanted to work at the home office as soon as possible, and now he has his chance."

"Yeah, that makes things tough for you," Christina agreed. "But there's nothing you can do. We need to pray about it."

Christina had just placed her hand on Mandy's shoulder when they heard the sound of Tony's office door opening. Both of them glanced up.

"Thanks, Uncle Ed," Tony said. "I'll think about everything and get back with you soon."

"Don't wait too long, Tony. In fact, I need an answer by the end of the month."

"That gives me two weeks."

Edward grinned at Mandy and Christina. "I'm happy to see that Small World is able to attract such good people. You made it easy for us to do what we need to do for company growth."

Tony spoke up. "Why don't you ladies go grab some lunch?" He pulled out his wallet, opened it, and handed Mandy some money. "If you don't mind, I'd like for you to bring me something back."

Mandy pushed the money back at him. "I'll treat."

Edward laughed as he whipped out some money. "No, I'll treat. Everyone, put your money back. This is on me."

"You don't need to buy our lunch," Mandy said.

"No, but I want to," Edward said as he took Mandy's hand and folded it around the money. "In fact, I'd like to join you ladies, if you don't mind. Cissy and Maria called a few minutes ago and said someone told them about a charming restaurant called Stratford Springs."

Mandy nodded. "They'll enjoy it."

Edward tilted his head. "Would you ladies like for me to take you there now? Cissy said they were heading there now, so we can join them."

"Um. . ." Mandy had some work to do, and it might take a while, but she didn't want to turn Edward down. She turned a pleading look toward Tony.

"I need her back here in less than an hour, and it might take a while to get there," Tony said.

Edward folded his arms as he made a contemplative face. "I understand. Maybe some other time."

"Sounds good," Mandy said.

"Why don't you join Mom and Cissy?" Tony asked. "I'm sure they'd like that."

With a nod, Edward walked toward the door. "Since you three have so much to do around here, I think I will."

After he left, Mandy let out a sigh. "Christina, let's go get some food." Then she turned to Tony. "What would you like us to bring you?"

He shrugged. "I'll eat anything you get."

æ

Tony couldn't help but notice the change in Mandy's attitude. She'd been so happy about the promotion, but now she was more subdued. He had a pretty good idea of what was bothering her. He'd have to talk to her after she and Christina finished with their afternoon appointments.

He was surprised when they walked in the door twenty minutes later. Mandy handed him one of the two bags she was holding. "We decided to eat here, since there's so much to do."

"All the more reason to get more people in here. That was a brilliant idea Christina had to hire seniors to make calls and staff the desk."

Mandy agreed. "My sister is very smart."

"It obviously runs in the family."

"Thank you." Mandy avoided his gaze as she backed out of his office.

After lunch, the photo sessions went smoothly. Tony took calls from people interested in working, and he booked some interviews. At the end of the day, he asked Mandy to stick around for a few minutes.

nineteen

"Come on in," Tony said.

Mandy hesitated at the door before going into his office. "You needed to see me?"

"I noticed how you changed after Uncle Ed mentioned bringing me back to Atlanta."

Bull's-eye. "Sorry." She swallowed hard. "So when are you leaving?"

"I'm not sure I am," he replied. "It all depends."

After waiting a couple of seconds, and he didn't answer, she decided to probe. "What does it depend on?"

He stood up, came around from behind his desk, and took her hand. "On us."

Mandy's heart thudded so hard, she was sure he could hear it. "What about us?" Her voice came out low and airy.

Tony let go of her hand. "This isn't the time or place to do this."

"Do what?" Mandy asked.

He narrowed his eyes and grinned. "You're good."

"Whatever. When do you plan to open up and tell me?"

He lifted her hand to his lips and kissed the back of her knuckle. "How about tonight?"

"What if I have plans?" She shot him a playful grin. "After all, it is rather short notice."

"If you have plans?" He gave her a mischievous look right back then set his jaw and narrowed his gaze. "Break 'em."

"Oh." Mandy couldn't think of a witty retort, so she dropped the act. "I don't have plans. Would you like to come over?"

"I have a better idea. I'll pick you up at seven. Wear something nice."

"Where are we going?"

Tony winked. "You'll find out soon enough."

Mandy realized she wasn't going to get anything out of him then, so she nodded. "So I'd better get moving, since I have to change into something nice."

Tony glanced at his watch. "Yeah, you'd better hurry up. I'll be at your door in forty-five minutes."

All the way to her apartment, Mandy thought about the possibilities. If she had her way, Tony would tell her he'd never be able to leave her, and he'd remain in Wheeling to be near her. Then her thoughts drifted back to when she first met him. He'd made it very clear that Wheeling, West Virginia, was a temporary stop for him on his way up the career ladder of his family's business. His very words: "If I hadn't taken time out to join the army, I'd be where I want to be right now."

As the memory sank in, Mandy's hope diminished. She'd known Tony long enough to fall in love with him. And long enough to know that when he wanted something, he'd do whatever it took to get it, as long as it didn't go against his faith. He most likely wanted to celebrate his dream job with Small World.

After Mandy got home, she forced herself to pull on her favorite dress and refresh her makeup. He'd said to wear something nice, and this was the nicest thing she owned. Too bad, after this, she'd be sad every time she wore it.

Tony arrived five minutes early. Mandy thought about how he was probably eager to talk about his promotion and ultimate move. She wanted to be happy for him, so she put on her best smile and opened the door.

He reached for her hand and slipped a corsage on her wrist. She tilted her head. "What's this all about? Are we going to a prom?"

With a chuckle, he shrugged. "Maybe." With a sweeping gesture, he said, "Ready to go?"

"Let me grab my purse."

As soon as they got in the car, he put a CD into the car stereo. As strains of instrumental Christian music played, Mandy studied Tony's profile in the dim light of dusk. Was it her imagination, or was he nervous?

"Where are we going?"

"You'll see." He made a couple of turns then headed straight for Oglebay Park.

"Why are we going to a park?" she asked. "You told me to dress up."

He lifted a finger to her lips. "Just relax, okay?"

She clamped her mouth shut and nodded. After all, she didn't see that she had any choice.

He found a parking spot and helped her out of the car. "Let's go over there," he said. "I'd like a nice view."

Mandy did as she was asked, being very careful with each step, since she'd worn her heels. "I just wish you'd warned me that I'd have to walk in the grass. I would have worn sneakers."

Tony smiled as he bent over and scooped her into his arms. He didn't say anything until they'd reached a place with a garden view, and he gently set her down. "I thought this would be perfect since you're prettier than any flower that has ever grown here."

Mandy playfully swatted at his shoulder. "Stop that. You're being silly."

Without another word, Tony turned her to face him, a serious look on his face. "Mandy, I've already told you I love you."

Her mind went blank. She wanted to say something, but nothing would come out.

"As you know, this opportunity with Small World is something I've wanted since I came back. Seven months ago, before I met you, I wouldn't have hesitated. But now, I can't imagine life without you."

Mandy swallowed hard as her thoughts swirled. "What are you going to do?"

He hesitated then reached into his pocket and pulled out a small black box. As he got down on one knee, Mandy's knees started to wobble, and she swayed.

Tony reached out to steady her and smiled. "I don't care where I live or what I do as long as I have you by my side. Mandy"—he opened the box, and a flash of brilliance defied the darkening sky—"will you be my wife?"

Mandy reached out and touched the ring then quickly drew back. "I—I don't know what to say."

He frowned and started to stand. "Um, I thought you might—"

Mandy gently pushed him back down. "Yes, I'll marry you, but what about the promotion? Both of our promotions?"

Tony remained on one knee as he placed the ring on her finger then stood to face her. "Ricco, Uncle Ed, and I discussed it. He said I can remain in Wheeling as a studio manager, and you'll work out of the office in this area."

"But I thought you had to go back to Atlanta. Your mom—"

He laughed. "I called her. When I told her what I planned to do, she said that was even better than having me back in Atlanta."

"Oh." Mandy couldn't help but smile, then she remembered something. "What about my sister? Wasn't she supposed to manage the studio?"

"That's the best part. I talked Uncle Ed into keeping the Wheeling studio open—at least for the time being. Christina has agreed to be the first manager in the new studio in the Ohio Valley Mall."

Mandy frowned. "Does she know about—this?" She held up her finger and pointed to the ring.

A sheepish look crossed his face. "Well. . .yeah. You're not mad, are you? I mean, I wanted to talk to your parents, and she was right there, and—"

She slowly shook her head. "No, I'm not mad at all."

Tony leaned over and kissed Mandy; then they turned to look at the flowers. After a couple of moments of silence, he tugged her toward the car. "C'mon. I have reservations for dinner at the Ihlenfeld Room." He chuckled as she wobbled toward the car. "If I'd known how difficult this would be for you, I wouldn't have asked you to dress up."

She lost her balance, and he caught her. She laughed. "Looks like I'm literally falling for you."

"And I'll always be there to catch you."

A Letter To Our Readers

Dear Reader:

In order that we might better contribute to your reading enjoyment, we would appreciate your taking a few minutes to respond to the following questions. We welcome your comments and read each form and letter we receive. When completed, please return to the following:

Fiction Editor
Heartsong Presents
PO Box 719
Uhrichsville, Ohio 44683

1. Did you enjoy reading *Portrait of Love* by Debby Mayne?
   ❑ Very much! I would like to see more books by this author!
   ❑ Moderately. I would have enjoyed it more if

   _____

   _____

   _____

2. Are you a member of **Heartsong Presents**? ❑ Yes ❑ No
   If no, where did you purchase this book? _____

   _____

3. How would you rate, on a scale from 1 (poor) to 5 (superior), the cover design? _____

4. On a scale from 1 (poor) to 10 (superior), please rate the following elements.

   ____ Heroine   ____ Plot
   ____ Hero   ____ Inspirational theme
   ____ Setting   ____ Secondary characters

5. These characters were special because? _____

_____

_____

6. How has this book inspired your life? _____

_____

_____

7. What settings would you like to see covered in future
   Heartsong Presents books? _____

_____

_____

8. What are some inspirational themes you would like to see
   treated in future books? _____

_____

_____

9. Would you be interested in reading other **Heartsong
   Presents** titles? ❏ Yes ❏ No

10. Please check your age range:
    ❏ Under 18   ❏ 18-24
    ❏ 25-34   ❏ 35-45
    ❏ 46-55   ❏ Over 55

Name _____

Occupation _____

Address _____

City, State, Zip _____

E-mail _____

OZARK WEDDINGS

3 stories in 1

Love disrupts the lives
of three women in the
Ozark Mountains.
Will these women dare
to take a chance at
romance?

Contemporary, paperback, 352 pages, 5¾₆" x 8"

_____

HEARTSONG
PRESENTS

If you love Christian romance...

$10.⁹⁹

You'll love Heartsong Presents' inspiring and faith-filled romances by today's very best Christian authors...Wanda E. Brunstetter, Mary Connealy, Susan Page Davis, Cathy Marie Hake, and Joyce Livingston, to mention a few!

When you join Heartsong Presents, you'll enjoy four brand-new, mass-market, 176-page books—two contemporary and two historical—that will build you up in your faith when you discover God's role in every relationship you read about!

Imagine...four new romances every four weeks—with men and women like you who long to meet the one God has chosen as the love of their lives...all for the low price of $10.99 postpaid.

To join, simply visit www.heartsong presents.com or complete the coupon below and mail it to the address provided.

Mass Market 176 Pages

YES! Sign me up for Heartsong!

NEW MEMBERSHIPS WILL BE SHIPPED IMMEDIATELY!
Send no money now. We'll bill you only $10.99 postpaid with your first shipment of four books. Or for faster action, call 1-740-922-7280.

NAME _____

ADDRESS_____

CITY_____ STATE _____ ZIP _____

MAIL TO: HEARTSONG PRESENTS, P.O. Box 721, Uhrichsville, Ohio 44683
or sign up at **WWW.HEARTSONGPRESENTS.COM**